"Your face is not repulsive to me,"

Joanna told Jake plainly. "You're far too sensitive about your scars. You've hidden from the world too long."

"So, if I put my face close to yours... like this—" Jake came nearer until she could see every pore in his flesh "— you wouldn't draw back from me?"

"No!" Joanna said, but when he was very near she did pull away. It was not his face but his nearness that frightened her and left her weak with the effort to resist touching him.

"Liar!" Clearly he misunderstood. "Let's try a more difficult demonstration," he said. At the sudden touch of his firm lips, Joanna's resistance faltered. What had begun as an attempt to discourage her deepened into passionate possession.

Was Jake merely testing her, or was his searing kiss full of genuine fire?

D0869118

Other titles by

ANNE MATHER
IN HARLEQUIN PRESENTS

Many of these titles, and other titles in the Harlequin
Romance series, are available at your local book-
seller. For a free catalogue listing all available
Harlequin Presents and Harlequin Romances, send
your name and address to:

HARLEQUIN READER SERVICE,
M.P.O. Box 707,
Niagara Falls, N.Y. 14302
Canadian address:
Stratford, Ontario, Canada N5A 6W2

ANNE MATHER

whisper of darkness

Harlequin Books

TORONTO • LONDON • NEW YORK • AMSTERDAM
SYDNEY • HAMBURG • PARIS • STOCKHOLM

Harlequin Presents edition published August 1980
ISBN 0-373-10376-X

Original hardcover edition published in 1980
by Mills & Boon Limited

Copyright © 1980 by Anne Mather. All rights reserved.
Philippine copyright 1980. Australian copyright 1980.
Except for use in any review, the reproduction or utilization of
this work in whole or in part in any form by any electronic,
mechanical or other means, now known or hereafter invented,
including xerography, photocopying and recording, or in any
information storage or retrieval system, is forbidden
without the permission of the publisher.

All the characters in this book have no existence outside the
imagination of the author and have no relation whatsoever to
anyone bearing the same name or names. They are not even
distantly inspired by any individual known or unknown to the
author, and all the incidents are pure invention.

The Harlequin trademark, consisting of the word HARLEQUIN
and the portrayal of a Harlequin, is registered in the United States
Patent Office and in the Canada Trade Marks Office.

Printed in U.S.A.

CHAPTER ONE

THE track to Ravengarth wound up over the rise, or so the bus driver had informed her, casting a rather amused glance at her high heels. It followed the contours of the low stone wall, narrow and pitted with tire tracks, and treacherously slippy after the rain the night before.

'There's no proper road to Ravengarth,' he had insisted, when she had protested she had been told otherwise, and the murmurings among the other passengers had convinced her that she was holding them up unnecessarily. She had climbed down, lugging her heavy suitcase behind her, and coughed in some resentment at its departing expulsion of fumes.

The road she was on was little more than a lane as it was. High hedges, thick with the fruits of autumn, hugged the ditches at either side, and the only sound after the bus had departed was the distant bleating of some sheep. It was remote, and isolated, and even slightly unnerving, a sensation Joanna was not at all used to feeling.

Stiffening her shoulders, she determinedly pushed such fanciful notions aside. There was no point in indulging in regrets. She was here. She had a job of work at last. And anything was better than the hand-to-mouth existence she and her mother had lived for the past six months.

Even so, as she began to climb the muddy track, sticking as close to the wall as she could to avoid the more obvious potholes, she couldn't help a wry grimace at the realisation of how ill-prepared she had been to face a situation like this. Who would have thought that her education at an exclusive girls' school, followed by an equally expensive sojourn at a finishing school in Switzerland, should have produced someone so evidently lacking in useful accomplishments? It was true that her shcooldays had been dogged by reports that read: 'Joanna is an intelligent girl, *but* she pays too little attention to her lessons.' Or: 'Joanna is very popular with her school friends, *but* she must spare more time for her studies.' Nevertheless, her results had been only a little below average, and what use were 'O' or 'A' levels to someone who was destined to marry into a wealthy family like her own, and whose main task in life would be the running of her husband's home?

At the top of the rise she stood for a moment, regaining her breath as she surveyed the distance she had yet to cover. The track wound down for a while, disappearing into a belt of trees, and beyond the trees she could vaguely see the chimneys of a house. That must be Ravengarth, she thought a little irritably. At least half a mile away. Couldn't they have sent someone to meet her? There were not that many buses that ran from Penrith to Ravensmere. Surely someone could have taken the trouble to find out what time her train arrived.

Realising there was no point in wasting time in silent imprecations, she picked up her case again and began to descend the downward track. Although the climb she had just undertaken had been harder, she soon realised it was easier to keep one's feet going up than coming down. Stones, seemingly embedded in mud, moved when she placed her foot upon them, and once or twice she had to snatch at the stone wall to keep her balance. Her temper was not improved by the knowledge that the mud would doubtless stain the navy blue suede of her boots, and it squelched sulkily beneath her, as if anticipating her eventual downfall.

By the time she reached the gate which opened into the copse, Joanna was hot and tired, and the autumn beauty of the surrounding hills made no impression on her irritated disposition. It was a cool September afternoon, and she had dressed accordingly in a belted coat of wine-dark suede over a sweater dress of a toning rose colour. Aunt Lydia had expressly said that she should be prepared for it being cooler in the Lake District, and she had taken her advice without question. Now, she felt she could have done without the warm clothing or the boots, though rubber boots would not have come amiss.

Beyond the gate, a notice reading: 'Private Land. Trespassers will be prosecuted' aroused only a moment's interest. Obviously Mr Sheldon did not encourage visitors, and remembering what Aunt Lydia had told her about him, perhaps it was understandable. He had chosen to hide himself away from the world, and obviously he would not welcome intruders.

The birds in the trees all around her were making their preparations for the night, and protested loudly as her feet crunched on fallen twigs and other debris, left by the previous night's rain. She supposed the lane was wide enough to take a Land Rover, and probably that was what one would need to get up that rutted track, but apparently Mr Sheldon's staff were not cosseted in that way, and Joanna's lips tightened as her case began to hang ever more heavily from her aching fingers.

Then two things happened so suddenly that seconds later the offending suitcase had fallen from her nerveless grasp. There was a shot, a distinct explosion of sound, that ricocheted round the copse with an ear-splitting blast that sent all the birds skyward in panic-stricken flight. Joanna knew how they felt. She wished she could escape in similar fashion. But instead she was forced to remain where she was, albeit shaking from the tips of her toes to the top of her head, and gaze at the diminutive figure that had sprung out of the trees just after the shot and now stood facing her in the middle of the track.

What was it? she asked herself, dry-mouthed, staring at the aggressive creature that confronted her, still gripping the smoking shotgun in its hand. No more than four and a half feet tall, dressed in filthy jeans and ragged sweater, a cap pulled down low over its eyes, she guessed it must be a poacher she had disturbed at his work, and judging by the size of him, little more than a boy.

Not that this reassured her. Nowadays children committed the most abominable crimes, and she was in no position to argue with a cartridge full of small shot. Somehow she had to convince him that she presented no threat to his livelihood, and to this end, she took a tentative step forward.

'Stay where y'are!'

The voice was pitched low, but its message was unmistakable, and Joanna licked her lips and tried again.

'I—if you'll get out of my way, I promise I won't mention having seen you,' she said, in what she hoped was her best and most convincing tone. 'Honestly, I'm not interested in what you're doing. I just want to get on my way——'

'—to Ravengarth,' finished the boy gruffly. 'Aye, I know all about that. But you can't go to Ravengarth. You're not welcome there. If I was you, I'd go back where I came from, before I point this gun in your direction.'

Joanna could hardly believe her ears. This simply could not be happening, she thought incredulously. Any minute now she would wake up to find Lottie by the bed with her breakfast tray, and Ravengarth and Jake Sheldon and his troublesome daughter would still be just an idea in Aunt Lydia's neatly coiffured head. Nightmares like this were an occupational hazard, and in a day or two she would find someone who welcomed her services, who did not require certificates and diplomas to prove that she could teach good manners to their small offspring, or handle the kind of correspondence she had been receiving herself for years.

But it was no nightmare. Without thinking she took another involuntary step forward, and the woods rang again with the deafening roar of the shotgun. It dispelled for ever the thought that this might not be happening, and Joanna stepped back quickly, tripped over her case, and sat down heavily on a mouldy pile of leaves.

What happened then shocked her almost as much as the shotgun had done. The child, for it was obviously nothing more, started laughing, shrill peals of merriment filled the air that was still trembling after the explosion, and amidst her fear, and the dismay at the ruination of her coat, a surge of angry suspicion swelled inside her. She tried desperately to recall exactly what Aunt Lydia had told her about Antonia Sheldon, but all she could remember was her age—eleven years—and the fact that she had succeeded in ridding herself of three governesses in as many months.

However, before she could struggle to her feet and put her suspicions to the test, another figure strode out of the woods behind the child, a tall, equally threatening figure in the gloom cast by the trees, who grasped the barrel of the shotgun in a powerful hand, wrenching it out of the child's grasp. At the same time, the man grabbed hold of the urchin before it could move, holding it securely by the scruff of the neck, as he transferred his attention to Joanna.

She, for her part, got to her feet with as much elegance as her shaking legs would permit her, brushing away the muddy leaves, and endeavouring to regain her composure. Aware of them watching her with varying degrees of hostility, she realised that until now she had not even speculated about the man who was to be her employer, but across the yards of track that separated them she was suddenly made aware that if this was he, he was not the prematurely-aged invalid she had imagined.

'Miss Seton?' The man was speaking now, ignoring the howling that had replaced the peals of laughter issuing from his prisoner's mouth, and she nodded. 'If you're not hurt, perhaps you'll follow me.'

Joanna gasped. That was it! No apology, no explanation; no offer to carry her suitcase that was as muddy now as her coat. He had simply turned away, propelling the screaming child ahead of him, the safely breached shotgun hooked over his free arm. Of course, he might have found some difficulty in handling the shotgun, the suitcase and the child, she acknowledged reasonably, but he didn't even offer any regret at this deficiency in his capabilities.

Clamping her jaws together, Joanna hoisted her suitcase once more and set off in pursuit of her apparently unwilling rescuer. To add to her weariness, her legs were decidedly unsteady now, and resentment flared anew at this cavalier treatment. She was doing them the favour, goodness knows, she muttered peevishly. She didn't *have* to come here. She didn't *have* to stay. And if this was the kind of treatment the other governesses had had, no wonder they hadn't stayed either!

They emerged from the trees above an incline, with a trout stream gurgling at its foot. Approximately halfway down the slope, the house she had glimpsed earlier clung tenaciously to the hillside, its grey walls mellowed by russet-coloured creeper. The track wound down to its stone gateposts, and set around the main building were stables and garages and the usual miscellany of outhouses. It was bigger that Joanna had expected, larger, but not so well-kept, and she wondered if they had the same problem with housekeepers as they had with governesses.

She had not yet seen the man's face clearly. In the shadows of the wood it had been impossible to glimpse more than an impression of his features, and besides, she had been too shocked and disturbed to pay much attention to his appearance. He was tall and powerful, lean without being thin, with strong muscular thighs that swung him down the track without any apparent effort. Was this Jake Sheldon? she wondered, struggling after him. Could it be? She would know soon enough if he turned and let her see the scars which Aunt Lydia had said had driven him to take refuge in this remote and isolated part of the country.

The child was something else. She found it incredible to believe that the uncouth demon of the copse was in reality an eleven-year-old *girl*! What was her father thinking of, allowing her to run around in that state, and with a loaded shotgun in her hand? She could have killed herself. She could have killed Joanna! And after all, that was the greater of the two evils so far as Joanna was concerned.

The child's cries had subsided to a muffled sobbing by the time they reached the gates of Ravengarth, but Joanna could not find it in her heart to feel sorry for her. She had to be crazy, brandishing a deadly weapon like that, and Joanna's belief in her own capabilities suffered a distinct setback at the prospect of teaching such a child.

A pair of long-haired sheepdogs set up a noisy barking at their approach, bounding out to greet them with more excitement than aggression. They fawned around their master and his charge for a moment, and then came to in-spect Joanna, apparently finding her equally acceptable. As watchdogs they were decidedly unprofessional, thought Joanna dryly, but as pets they were adorable.

The man let go of the child as they entered a gloomy entrance hall, unpleasantly scented with the smell of boiled cabbage, and administering a distinct slap to her small backside, bade her go and make herself respectable immediately. Then, as she scampered towards the stairs that curved round two walls of the hall, he turned sharply into a room on his left, asking Joanna to follow him.

Joanna did so, after setting down her suitcase with great relief. As she straightened, however, her eyes again encountered those of the child now leaning dangerously far over the banister rail, and the impudent contempt in that stare made her long to repeat the punishment her father had given, with interest. If she had to take this job, and in spite of her vain posturings she hadn't much alternative, sooner or later Miss Sheldon would have to understand she was no longer dealing with some timid, self-effacing old lady.

The room into which her employer—she *assumed* he was her employer—led her was a library of sorts, although many of the shelves were empty of books, their places having been taken by folders of what appeared to be artwork. There were canvases everywhere, propped against the walls, and the bookcases, some even occupied the chairs where possible, and others were spread across the heavy mahogany desk that sat squarely beneath the long windows. The air was musky with the smell of oils, and faintly stale from the neglected shelves of books.

The man positioned himself beside the desk, deliberately, Joanna later decided. There was not much light from the overcast sky, but what there was fell fully on to his scarred and battered countenance, and she was left in no doubt that this was indeed Jake Sheldon.

'Well?' he said, as if challenging her with his appearance. 'It's not a pretty sight, is it? But then you knew that, didn't you? Someone must have told you—have *warned* you.'

Joanna wondered if anyone had ever had a more peculiar introduction to a job. A child, who dressed and spoke and behaved like a boy—a particularly objectionable boy at that—and a man who had apparently been deprived of his manners in the same accident in which he had been deprived of his livelihood. They had said he was a brilliant mathematician, a skilled and accomplished engineer, a man with a computer for a brain. And what was he now? An indifferent farmer, a part-time painter, and the father of a child who was evidently free to do exactly as she liked.

And he was challenging her to dispute his appearance, to deny that it shocked her feminine sensitivities. His face was scarred, it was true, but it was by no means repugnant, and she wondered if he realised how time had mellowed old wounds and given his ravaged face a certain strength and character. Some women might even find his rugged features attractive, and Joanna realised that Aunt Lydia and her mother could have had no idea of how old he actually was. Aunt Lydia's description had been vague at best, and because he had a nineteen-year-old son she had evidently assumed he was well into middle age. But Joanna, facing him in that revealing light, saw that he was probably on the right side of forty, and this was going to prove a most unsuitable arrangement if no other help was kept. If his expression had not been so grimly serious, she might have allowed a small smile to tilt the corners of her mouth, but the situation was still far too volatile to take such liberties.

'Cat got your tongue?' he enquired now, cynically, turning from the window to flick through the canvases on the desk, and she endeavoured to gather her thoughts.

'My godmother told me you required someone to take care of your daughter,' she ventured at last. 'I assume that was your daughter who—greeted me on my arrival.'

His lower lip jutted as he surveyed her slightly dishevelled appearance. It was a full lower lip; it might even be called sensual. And Joanna was given the piercing appraisal of narrowed amber eyes.

'I suppose I should apologise for Antonia, shouldn't I?' he remarked, as if considering the proposition, and the disarming amusement which had briefly dispelled her indignation vanished.

'Perhaps she should apologise for herself?' she retorted, controlling her resentment with difficulty. 'And I would suggest she is forbidden to run wild with firearms in future.'

His shoulders stiffened. 'Oh, you would, would you?'

'Yes.' Joanna drew herself up to her full height, but even then her five feet six inches fell far short of his superior measure. 'I don't think that's an unreasonable request. She could have killed me in the woods. Obviously she doesn't understand——'

'She understands very well,' he interrupted her harshly, the dark brows descending with ominous intent. 'She's known how to handle guns for the past two years—I taught her. You were in no danger.' He paused, allowing his astonishing words to sink in. 'You were, however, subjected to a certain amount of—intimidation.'

'Intimidation! Is that what you call it?' Joanna could feel the colour sweeping up her normally pale cheeks. 'How was I to know who she was or what she was doing? She was filthy. She was wearing boy's clothes. She could have been a thief—a poacher, disturbed at his work!'

'I see you have a vivid imagination, Miss Seton. That's—unfortunate. I would have preferred someone a little more —unimaginative.'

His hesitation before using that particular adjective was deliberate, Joanna felt, pinpointing as it did his evident opinion of her. She had never encountered such indifference from a man before, or experienced such a feeling of blind frustration. She didn't know exactly what she had anticipated, but certainly nothing like this, and his defence of the child was in complete opposition to his expected reaction. She felt like flinging his job back in his face, and only the thought of her mother's disappointment if she returned to London without giving it a chance kept her silent.

'So,' he said, indicating an upright chair opposite. 'Won't you sit down, and we can discuss the situation more—amicably. I understand from my sister that you haven't had any actual experience of teaching a child before, and that you have in fact been finding it hard to gain employment.'

Joanna sat down on the chair he indicated with a bump. He was certainly frank, she thought indignantly, or perhaps insolent was a better description of his vaguely mocking turn of phrase. In the space of a few sentences he had dismissed her claims of being physically threatened, and reduced her qualifications to nil.

'I never expected to have to get a job, Mr Sheldon,' she declared now, holding up her head in icy disdain. 'Until my father's death——'

'Yes, I know,' he interrupted unpleasantly, tumbling a pile of canvases on to the floor and taking the seat behind the desk. 'You were a lady of leisure—I had heard. However, I'm not interested in how you came to be looking for a job, rather the accomplishments you have which make you think you are capable of teaching an eleven-year-old.'

Joanna gazed at him, not quite able to hide her astonishment. Did he really think he could speak to her like that, employee or otherwise? How dared he sit here in this run-down house, making excuses for a child who was little more than a barbarian, so far as Joanna could see, and expect her to be grateful for his indulgence in even listening to her? However dismayed her mother might be, surely she would not expect her daughter to be subjected to such treatment.

Grasping the strap of her handbag, Joanna rose to her feet. 'I don't think the accomplishments I possess fit me for this position at all, Mr Sheldon,' she declared coldly. 'We have obviously both been under some misapprehension about the other. I expected to have to teach a—a little girl, not an uncontrollable adolescent, and if I was prepared to make allowances for the child, I'm certainly not prepared to make allowances for its father!'

If she expected her remarks to arouse some answering retort from him, she was very much mistaken. And while remorse at the recklessness of such a declaration, influenced as it was by the lateness of the hour and a reluctant awareness of her own unfamiliarity with either the area or its transport services, caused her no small anxiety, Jake Sheldon sat there, gazing up at her, a look of sardonic amusement twisting his hard features.

'You think I'm an ignorant savage, don't you?' he asked at last. 'You'd like very much to tell me what I can do with my job. But from what I hear, you don't have a great deal of choice.'

Joanna gulped. 'I can get another job, Mr Sheldon.'

'Can you?'

He pushed back his own chair now and stood up, dark and intimidating in the rapidly fading light. It was obviously later than she had thought, and the prospect of making her way back to the road and possibly having to thumb a lift back to Penrith was a daunting one. But she would not stay here to be insulted, not by a man who in his rough shirt and waistcoat and mud-splattered corded pants looked more like a gipsy than anything else.

'I suggest, Miss Seton, that you reconsider,' he said now. 'Perhaps I was—hard on you, but you have to understand, it's over two years since I had any—*polite* conversation. As to your abilities to teach Anya, that's something we have both to consider. However, I'm prepared to give you the benefit of the doubt, provided you are prepared to do the same.'

It was scarcely an apology. On the contrary, it was more in the nature of a concession, as if he was overlooking her insolence.

'I really don't think I can stay here, Mr Sheldon,' she insisted, glancing round at the shabby chairs, the equally shabby carpet. 'I—well, I was misinformed. Your sister told my godmother that your daughter needed eighteen months' preparation for boarding school. Having seen the child for myself, I suggest her estimate was vastly underrated.'

'The challenge is too much for you, then?' he remarked scornfully. 'I had heard you had spirit, the only evident point in your favour. Apparently that was *over*rated.'

Joanna's lips compressed, torn by the conflicting desire to prove to this man that he was wrong, and the conviction that she should leave now before any further humiliation was heaped upon her.

As she hesitated, groping for words, there was a tap on

the half-open door behind her, and a slovenly-looking woman appeared in the aperture. Jake Sheldon seemed resigned, but not impatient, at the interruption, and arched black brows above those startling tawny eyes.

'Yes, Mrs Harris?'

'What time will you be wanting your supper, sir,' she enquired, casting a look of avid curiosity in Joanna's direction, so that she was firmly convinced that was the only reason the woman had appeared. 'Anya's tucking into hers in the kitchen, right this minute, but I wondered whether you and the—er—young lady——'

'Anya's doing *what*!'

The thunderous tones obviously cowed the cook—housekeeper?—as much as they shocked Joanna. With a muffled oath her would-be employer strode angrily across the room, disappearing out the door without a backward glance. It was left to Joanna to exchange an awkward glance with Mrs Harris, and they both waited in anxious anticipation for what would happen next.

They did not have long to wait. Seconds later, the silence was broken by a scream of indignation, and two pairs of footsteps could be heard approaching from the kitchens, and then receding up the stairs. These sounds were accompanied by more of the choking sobs Anya had emitted earlier, and the low harsh admonishment of Jake Sheldon's not unattractive tones.

Mrs Harris waited until they were out of earshot, and then said confidentially: 'A proper tearaway, that young Anya is, and no mistake. What's she done now? Why was Mr Sheldon so angry, just 'cos she was having her supper?'

Joanna licked her dry lips. 'I—I really don't know,' she lied, wishing perversely that Jake Sheldon would hurry and come back, and Mrs Harris's bony arms folded across her flat bosom.

'You going to stay then?' she enquired, apparently determined to make the most of her employer's absence. 'I shouldn't, if I was you. No place for a nicely brought up young lady, this isn't. And if you expect to make any headway with that limb of Satan,' she dipped her head significantly in the direction of the door, 'then you can think again. Three ladies there've been, real nice ladies, like yourself. Maybe a bit older, but all with proper qualifications, you know. All gone! Every one of them. Wouldn't put up with that besom for more than a couple of weeks at a time. Drummed out of school, she was. Been to four schools since she and her father came here, but none of them would keep her. Troublemaker, that's what they said, nothing but trouble——'

'Really, Mrs—Harris, is it?' Joanna had to stop her somehow, 'I don't think you ought to be telling me all this. I—er—if I decide not to stay, it won't be because of anything you've said.'

'But you are thinking of it, then?' Mrs Harris had heard the note of indecision in her voice. 'Don't blame you. Living in this Godforsaken place.'

She pronounced God as *Gawd*, obviously in no way offended by Joanna's attempt to silence her. She was a garrulous old gossip, and Joanna's mother wouldn't have had her in the house for more than five minutes, but apparently Jake Sheldon had no such misgivings.

'Mrs Harris ...' Joanna was beginning again, when heavy footsteps sounded once more on the stairs. Evidently Mr Sheldon was returning, and her voice trailed away as he strode back into the room.

'You may leave us, Mrs Harris,' he said shortly, seemingly irritated to find her still there. 'You can serve supper in half an hour. Whether Miss Seton chooses to join me or not is immaterial. Lay a place, just in case.'

'Yes, sir.'

The woman cast another glance in Joanna's direction, before going out of the room. Her look was speculative, as if she was mentally calculating whether Joanna would tell her employer what she had been saying, but there was no apprehension in her gaze. Obviously she was not afraid of losing her position, and Joanna could only assume that she had good reason for feeling secure.

With the older woman's departure, Jake Sheldon's gaze turned to Joanna once again, and there was weariness as well as impatience in his expression now.

'Well?' he said. 'Do I take it you've decided to leave? If so, then I'd better run you into Ravensmere in the Rover. I believe there's a bus to Penrith in half an hour. I doubt you'll get a train to London tonight, but the Station Hotel will likely find you a room.'

Joanna hesitated. 'The child—Antonia; where is she?'

'In bed,' he declared indifferently. 'Nursing her pride, I imagine.'

'You hit her?' Joanna couldn't keep the note of unease out of her voice.

'She had it coming,' he replied laconically. 'And if you're feeling guilty because of it, forget it. Please don't imagine it places you under any obligation to stay.'

Joanna sighed. 'I don't know what to do.'

'No?' He sounded sceptical. 'I should have thought after what Mrs Harris must have told you, you'd have been standing on the doorstep, your suitcase in your hand.'

'Mrs Harris never——' But after a moment, Joanna broke off, realising there was no point in lying to him. 'That is—I don't listen to gossip.'

'Don't you?' He shrugged his broad shoulders rather jadedly. 'You mean you didn't hear about the other governesses who have tried and failed to discipline my daughter, or the numerous schools I've sent Anya to in an effort to improve her education.'

Joanna frowned. 'Why do you call her Anya? I understood her name was Antonia.'

'It is.' He sounded bored with the conversation, but he explained. 'When she was just learning to talk, she couldn't say her own name. The consonant was beyond her. She used to call herself An-ia. We—that is, my wife and I—used to call her that, too, and over the years it's been turned into Anya.'

'I see.' It had been a silly question in the circumstances, and Joanna felt rather embarrassed now.

'Having disposed of that, I suggest you make up your mind what you're going to do. It's getting late, and I have work to do.'

'I'm sorry.' Joanna almost choked on the apology. What a boor of a man he was! There ought not to be a shred of hesitation in her rejection of his offer, and yet for some reason she was loath to give him that satisfaction. He thought she was frivolous, useless; an ornament, finding the utilitarian world a cold and barren place. She would like the chance to prove to him that this was not so, that she could play just as useful a role in society as anyone else. And to have that chance, she had to ignore all the rudeness and insults he put in her way, and demonstrate her ability to succeed in spite of him.

However, he seemed to have taken her apology as a clear rejection of the position he was offering her. Without another word he had crossed the thinly carpeted floor towards the door, and only her instinctive: 'Mr Sheldon!' caused him to pause and look at her.

'Yes?'

Joanna's tongue circled her lips once more. 'I—I'll stay,' she said impulsively, and immediately wished that she had not.

'You will?' There was a glimmer of relief in the narrowed eyes, but that was all. No great enthusiasm, no words of encouragement or gratitude. Just 'You will?' followed by a perfunctory: 'I'll get Mrs Harris to show you your room.'

'No!' Joanna took an involuntary step forward, and then felt herself colouring, something she had not done in ages. 'I—that is, couldn't you just tell me where I'm to sleep? I'm sure I could find my own way. Without—without troubling Mrs Harris.'

'As you wish.' He seemed to be mentally washing his hands of the whole affair. 'It's the third door on the right at the top of the stairs. If you'll leave your suitcase, I'll carry it up later.'

'I can manage,' mumbled Joanna unwillingly, biting her tongue against the remark that if she could carry it fully a mile from the bus stop, she could certainly carry it up a few stairs, and he made a dismissive gesture.

'Very well. But I suggest you leave your unpacking until

after supper. Mrs Harris's meals are best taken hot, and you'll have plenty of time later to get accustomed to your surroundings.'

Joanna inclined her head. Evidently one did not change for dinner at Ravengarth. She wondered if Jake Sheldon intended to come to the table in the same disreputable gear he was wearing at the moment. It seemed highly likely, and a small voice inside her evinced mild hysteria at her decision to stay. She must be mad, she thought, after Jake Sheldon had left her and she was climbing the stairs. No one should have to pay so heavily just to prove one's point.

CHAPTER TWO

It was a curious evening, a slightly unreal evening, and lying in bed later that night, Joanna reviewed its events with a certain amount of incredulity. It had definitely not resembled any first evening she might have anticipated, and the feeling of anticlimax she had experienced had not yet dissipated.

Her bedroom, which she had found no difficulty in locating, was quite a spacious apartment, but its appearance matched the rest of the house. Either Jake Sheldon had no money to spend on refurbishment, or he simply didn't care about his surroundings. The wallpaper was old, and peeling in places where the furniture had been pushed against the walls, the floor's only covering was linoleum, which would be icy cold to the feet on winter mornings, and the furniture itself would not have disgraced a junkyard. Joanna had been at first appalled, and then amazed, and finally reluctantly amused to find herself in such a situation.

The view from her windows made up in some part for the rest. Although it was getting dark, it was still possible to glimpse the tumbling beauty of the stream, and beyond, the glimmer of a larger expanse of water. In the distance the shadowy fells brooded, dark and mysterious, casting a sheltering arm around the stillness of the valley.

Taking Jake Sheldon's advice, Joanna had paused only long enough to wash her face at the handbasin she found in her room and apply some fresh make-up before going downstairs. Her hair, despite her ordeal, was still secure in its knot, and the jersey dress was not unwelcome now as the evening grew cooler. There was an ancient radiator in her room, she noticed, but it was stone cold at present, and she wondered if such an antiquated plumbing system was still operational. If not, it was going to be very cold on winter mornings, with only open fires to provide any heat.

However, she refused to consider something so nebulous as the future. Right now, she had the present to live with, and despite her determination it was a daunting task she had set herself.

Downstairs again, she found the dining room by means of trial and error. There was no one about, and she glimpsed a sitting room and a cloakroom before finding a room with a table laid for one. This in itself was puzzling enough, but Mrs Harris, who appeared a few moments later, explained in her usual garrulous way that Mr Sheldon would not be taking supper after all.

'He's had to go down to the village after Matt Coulston,' she confided, setting a plate of thick soup in front of Joanna. 'Been drinking since opening time, he has, and George Page at the Fox and Hounds can't handle him.'

Joanna picked up her spoon. She was reluctant to ask questions of the housekeeper, but if she was going to live here she would have to know who everyone was, and with a reluctant sigh she ventured: 'Mr Coulston works for Mr Sheldon?'

''Course he does.' Mrs Harris stood back from the table, and nodded her greying head. 'Sort of shepherd and general handyman he is, when he's sober.'

'Isn't it a little early in the evening for anyone to be—intoxicated?' Joanna asked doubtfully, but Mrs Harris only laughed, a rather unpleasant gurgling cackle, that split her thin lips and displayed a dearth of teeth in her lower jaw.

'When Matt goes on one of his binges, time doesn't have anything to do with it,' she declared with a sniff. 'He'll have been drinking since early this morning, and by now he'll be roaring drunk. There's only Mr Sheldon can handle him at times like that, but he'll get him back to his cottage and lock him in until he sobers up.'

'I see.' Joanna took her first mouthful of the soup and managed to hide her distaste as its powdery consistency clung to the roof of her mouth. 'Well—thank you, Mrs Harris. I—er—I'll have to eat alone.'

For an awful moment after she'd uttered those words, Joanna wondered if the housekeeper would imagine they were some kind of an invitation, but apparently Mrs Harris had other things on her mind.

'You're staying, then?' she probed, lingering by the door. 'Or is he just putting you up for the night, until you can get a train back to London?'

Joanna was tempted to say it was none of her business, but that would have been unreasonable. After all, Mrs Harris had to cater for the household, though judging by the state of the place her ministrations were by no means satisfactory.

'I'm staying,' she replied now, taking another mouthful of soup after surreptitiously stirring it with her spoon. 'At least for the present. I hope I may have more success than those ladies had.'

'Some hopes,' muttered Mrs Harris dourly, and Joanna looked up.

'You sound pessimistic, Mrs Harris. Anyone would think you didn't want me to succeed.'

'Oh, no. No,' the housekeeper denied this hastily. 'O' course, I hope you're successful. It's just that—well, Anya's not like an ordinary child, if you know what I mean. Been too much with adults, she has——'

'I think you should leave me to learn about—Anya—for myself,' replied Joanna firmly, cutting her off. 'This soup is very nice. What are you going to offer me as an entrée, I wonder?'

Mrs Harris frowned, screwing up her mouth. 'I don't know what you mean by no on-tree,' she declared, sniffing again. 'But there's lamb chops to follow, and a piece of my custard.'

Joanna endeavoured to appear enthusiastic, and to her relief Mrs Harris took her dismissal. But as the meal progressed, she began to understand why Jake Sheldon had suggested that Mrs Harris's meals were best taken hot. Lamb was a greasy dish at any time, and in Mrs Harris's unskilled hands it had been allowed to swim in its own fat. Left to go cold, it would be revolting, and she wondered whether her employer would be expected to eat it later. The vegetables, boiled carrots and potatoes, had fared a little better, but the gravy, like the soup earlier, was inclined to be floury. The custard tart to finish was not set properly, and as she sat over a cup of instant coffee, which anyone could make, Joanna wondered if the housekeeper would object to being given a few tips. Cooking was one of Joanna's few accomplishments, and although in the past it had been confined to preparing sauces and desserts for far more elaborate meals, she didn't think she could do much worse than the unfortunate Mrs Harris.

With supper over, she wandered aimlessly into the sitting room, switching on the standard lamp by the window, and drawing the heavy repp curtains. She discovered a rack of paperback books in an alcove, and a pile of outdated science magazines, and the furnishings were completed by a pair of buttoned horsehair sofas, that gave as liberally as a saddle when one sat upon them, and a black and white television set. Two corner cupboards faced the wide fireplace, but their contents of chipped and dusty porcelain inspired only a fleeting interest. There were no dolls in evidence, no toys at all that she could see, except a couple of jigsaw puzzles, stuffed into the bottom of the bookcase. None of the items present in the room seemed to reflect Jake Sheldon's personality, and Joanna wondered whether he had bought—or leased?—the property already furnished. That would account for its deplorable lack of taste, she thought, although why she should imagine Jake Sheldon might have any taste was not a proposition she cared to explore.

Picking up one of the paperback books, she attempted to glean some interest in the activities of a well-known private detective, but her ears were constantly alert for any sound of her employer's return, and the events being described in the book seemed far less improbable than her own situation. She wondered if there was a phone so that she could ring her mother, but the idea of assuring her of her daughter's well-being seemed totally ludicrous in the present circumstances, and she decided to wait and write when she felt less emotional than she did at present.

She guessed she must have fallen asleep on the sofa,

despite its hardness, because when she next looked at the clock on the stone mantelpiece, it was after ten o'clock. She thought some sound must have wakened her, but she was still alone in the room, and inclined to be chilly because of the lowering of her body temperature during her nap.

She got stiffly off the couch and walked to the door into the hall, but there was no one about, and a frown furrowed her brow. She supposed she might as well go to bed as wait here indefinitely for her employer to appear, and with a feeling of flatness she went up the stairs to her room.

It was only as she opened the bedroom door that a sudden thought struck her. She had neither seen nor heard from Antonia all evening, and while her father had declared she was safely in bed, remembering the incident in the woods, Joanna couldn't help but feel apprehensive. She had read books about naughty children who upset suitcases and squeezed out toothpaste and even put lizards in their governesses' beds. While she had been lazily snoozing downstairs, Antonia—or Anya—could quite easily have wrought havoc up here.

She pushed open the door tentatively, half prepared to step back if some awful booby trap was waiting for her, but after groping for the switch and turning the light on, she found no apparent signs of mayhem. On the contrary, the room was exactly as she had left it, and she breathed a sigh of relief as she closed the door.

She undressed quickly, shivering as she put on the nightgown she had rummaged out of her case. The rest of her belongings could wait until the morning to be unpacked, she decided firmly, and after a speedy trip to the bathroom she climbed eagerly between the sheets.

The mattress was at least interior sprung, but the nap she had had downstairs had left her wide awake now that she wanted to fall asleep. She tossed and turned incessantly, wondering about Antonia, wondering whether she ought to have checked on the child to see if she was all right before going to bed, wondering whether Jake Sheldon would expect her to be waiting up for him whatever time he chose to come back. She finally fell into a fitful slumber that was rudely destroyed by someone drawing back the curtains and shaking her awake.

'What is it? What time is it?' she mumbled, not really conscious of her whereabouts as she struggled to push off the bony hand, and Mrs Harris's face swam before her, maliciously amused in the bright sunlight streaming in through the windows.

'It's time you was up, Miss Seton,' the housekeeper declared, setting down a cup of tea on the bedside table and folding her arms, a favourite position of hers. 'After eight o'clock, it is, and Mr Sheldon said to tell you we don't keep town hours here.'

'After eight o'clock ...' Joanna elbowed herself up on to her pillows, aware that Mrs Harris was studying her with evident interest. It made her self-consciously aware of the brevity of her silk nightgown, and also reminded her that this was the first time the housekeeper had seen her hair loose. Long and honey-brown, streaked with gold in places, it swung soft and becomingly about her shoulders, framing the oval shape of her face and accentuating the creamy paleness of her skin.

'Yes, nearly quarter past, it is, and if I was you I'd get myself downstairs.'

'Eight o'clock's not so late, is it?' protested Joanna, draping the sheet protectively about her shoulders. Despite the brightness of the day outside it was still chilly, and she needed a few minutes to gather her confused senses.

'Mr Sheldon had his breakfast at seven o'clock,' retorted Mrs Harris with evident relish. 'And I have other things to do than keep meals hanging about for hours.' She moved towards the door: 'It'll be on the table in fifteen minutes. If you're there, all well and good, if not——'

'Wait!' Joanna strove to get into a sitting position. 'Mrs Harris, I don't eat breakfast. At least, perhaps toast and coffee sometimes.' The aroma of frying bacon was unmistakable as the housekeeper opened the door. 'I'm afraid I can't stomach fried food in the mornings.'

Mrs Harris pursed her lips. 'You mean to say my fried eggs, sausages and bacon are going to be wasted?'

Joanna tried to hide her grimace. 'I'm sorry.' She was tempted to add, give them to the dogs, but she was glad she decided against it when Mrs Harris continued:

'I'll have to tell Mr Sheldon about this,' she declared, with the inevitable sniff. 'He can't afford for good food to go to waste. Like as not, he'll suggest that I warm it up for your lunch, so don't imagine you can pick and choose here like you used to in London.'

The door closed behind her, and Joanna's shoulders sagged. She wondered whether Mrs Harris would believe her if she told her that at home finances had been so tight that the idea of having bacon, eggs and sausages for breakfast would have been an unthinkable extravagance. It was true, she had never eaten a big breakfast, but that was mostly because at boarding school the food had been so appalling, and in Switzerland she had grown accustomed to the continental style of eating.

Still, there was no time now to sit and reflect on the past. Evidently she was expected to start work at nine o'clock, and it would probably take her half the time she had to pull herself together.

The cup of tea helped, despite the fact that it was thick and black, and far too sweet for her taste. But at least it was restoring, and she got out of bed afterwards with a little more enthusiasm.

The lino was icy to her toes, which certainly quickened her actions. Slipping her feet into slippers, she padded over to the washbasin, and after sluicing her face in lukewarm water and cleaning her teeth, she hastily put on the first things that came to hand. The purple corded jeans were blessedly warm, and she found a matching polo-necked sweater that dispelled the gooseflesh from her arms.

Her hair presented more of a problem, but she managed to coil it into a loose-fitting knot, although she was aware that the tendrils which persisted in falling about her ears gave it a far too casual appearance. Nevertheless, it would have to do until later, she decided, after an anxious examination of her watch, and after applying a shiny lipstick she hurriedly descended the stairs.

Once again she had the dining room to herself, the early sun highlighting the dents and stains that marked the heavy sideboard, and reflecting off windows grimy with the dust of months. However Mrs Harris filled her time, it was not in housework, thought Joanna grimly, realising that her mother would have dismissed the woman the minute she saw this place.

A congealing mess of bacon, sausages and broken eggs was set for Joanna's inspection, and she heaved a sigh of impatience. She had explained she didn't want the fried food, but the housekeeper had ignored her instructions. There was also toast—cold, she discovered, and *tea* instead of coffee.

It was too much. With a feeling of intense frustration, Joanna marched to the door, then stepped back in confusion as she almost collided with her employer. This morning he had not shaved as yet, and the shadow of his beard darkened his already swarthy skin. His black hair, and it was black, she saw, although streaked with grey in places, was rumpled, as if he had been threading his fingers through it, and he seemed to be wearing the same clothes as he had worn the night before. His scarred appearance seemed more obvious this morning, accentuated as it was by gauntness and exhaustion and a certain red-rimmed weariness about his eyes. She wondered for an awful moment whether he had joined the notorious Matt Coulston in his drinking bout, but there was no slurring of Jake Sheldon's speech when he said harshly: 'So you've decided to get up at last, Miss Seton. When you've had your breakfast, perhaps you and I could have a few words.'

Joanna glanced back at the table, and then took a deep breath. 'As a matter of fact, I wanted to have a few words with you, Mr Sheldon,' she stated, refusing to be intimidated by his grim countenance. 'I'm afraid I don't eat a cooked breakfast. I never have, and what's more, I prefer coffee in the mornings, not tea.'

'Oh, you do, do you?' His expression had not changed, though she perceived a faint hardening of the curiously cat-like eyes. 'Well, perhaps you ought to take that up with

Mrs Harris. She's the housekeeper around here, not me.'

'Is she?' mumbled Joanna, under her breath, but he had heard her, and the dark brows descended.

'What is that supposed to mean?'

Joanna sighed. The last thing she wanted this early in their association was an argument about his housekeeping arrangements, and bending her head, she moved her shoulders in an offhand gesture.

'Nothing,' she said at last. 'I—er—I'll speak to Mrs Harris, as you say.'

He seemed loath to leave it, though without her contribution he had no choice, but as he turned away she ventured: 'When will—er—Antonia be ready to start her lessons, Mr Sheldon? And where would you like me to conduct them?'

His frown was penetrating. A narrow concentration that made her wish she had waited for him to broach the subject. 'You don't know?' he demanded. 'Mrs Harris didn't tell you?'

'Tell me? Tell me what?'

'Anya ran away yesterday evening. I've been out all night looking for her.'

'No!' Joanna was horrified. That explained the haggard appearance, the growth of beard on the jawline. 'And have you found her? Do you know where she is? You should have woken me, I could have helped you.'

'Really?' His tone was sardonic. 'When you're the reason she ran away?'

Joanna flushed. 'Have you found her?'

He heaved a heavy sigh. 'I have a good idea where she is.'

'Where?'

He hesitated, as if reluctant to discuss it with her, and then he shrugged. 'There's a shepherd's hut, up on the fell. I know she goes there sometimes. It's about two miles from here, but until the mist lifts we haven't a hope in hell of finding it.'

'You knew that—last night?'

'I guessed, after searching the woods around the house,

and enquiring in the village.'

'Then why didn't you——'

'—go searching the fell?' He shook his head. 'You don't know this area very well, do you, Miss Seton? When the mist comes down, and at this time of the year it inevitably does, the fells are treacherous to an inexperienced climber like me. Even the rescue teams can't turn out in weather like that. They have to wait till the mist clears, till they can see where they're going.'

Joanna glanced towards the windows. 'But it's clear now.'

'It's clearing,' he agreed heavily. 'As soon as I've changed my clothes, I'm going out after her. I only hope to God she got there in time.'

Joanna made a helpless gesture. 'But—staying out all night!' She recalled the anxious moments she had had climbing the stairs the night before, the anticipation of childish pranks meant to deter her from staying. And all the while Antonia had not even been in the house. She felt hopelessly inadequate to combat such determination. 'Wouldn't she be afraid?'

'Anya?' There was pride as well as anxiety in his voice now. 'She's not afraid of the dark, if that's what you mean. And Binzer's with her, wherever she is. He won't leave her.'

'Binzer?' Joanna paused. 'That's a dog?'

'One of the sheepdogs you saw yesterday,' Jake agreed, expelling his breath wearily. 'And now, if you'll excuse me——'

'May I come with you?' Joanna's cheeks burned briefly as she encountered his sardonic gaze. 'I mean—to find Antonia, of course.'

'Call her Anya. Everybody does,' he remarked flatly. 'It may help you to get through to her, although I doubt it somehow.'

'And may I? Come with you?'

'Do you have any strong walking shoes?'

Joanna glanced down at the plain pumps she had worn for comfort. Obviously they were not suitable. 'I have some desert boots,' she murmured doubtfully.

'Desert boots?' He shook his head. 'What are they?'

'They're suede; ankle boots. They're quite strong.'

He looked at her for a disturbing moment, making her overwhelmingly aware of his opinion of her. She could almost feel his contempt scraping over her skin, and she realised how similar their situations were. He didn't really want a young female, with no formal qualifications, teaching his daughter. He would much have preferred one of the educated ladies Mrs Harris had spoken of, whose references were no doubt exemplary. And she had never expected to find herself in this position, being forced to care for a problem child, when what she had really hoped for was some pleasant sinecure with a wealthy family, where she could continue to live the kind of life to which until recently she had been accustomed.

'Very well,' he said at last, striding towards the stairs. 'Be ready in ten minutes. And bring a warm coat.'

The ten minutes gave her little time to eat any breakfast, or to complain about the choice of beverage. Instead, she scraped butter and jam on a slice of toast and carried it up to her room, deciding that now was not the time to cross swords with Mrs Harris.

The unmade bed gave the room an unkempt appearance, and after lacing on her boots she quickly shook the pillows and pulled up the covers. She doubted Mrs Harris would consider bed-making part of her duties, and as she had a couple of minutes to spare she contemplated a hasty appraisal of Anya's room. Maybe if she could see her belongings, the things she cared about, she would have some idea of how to approach her, and swallowing the last morsel of toast, she left her room. In the hall outside she slid her arms into the sheepskin jacket she was carrying, and made a swift inspection of the doors available to her. Apart from her door, and the door into the bathroom, there were four other doors, and her brow furrowed as she realised she had no way of knowing which was the child's room.

Biting her lip, she moved along the hall to the landing, and then glanced back. She guessed the two doors at the far side of the landing were more likely to be Jake Sheldon's doors than any of the others, and on impulse she moved closer to the first of the remaining doors, and put her ear to the panels. The doors were old, however, and very thick, and she doubted she would hear anything through them. But like all old doors, they had keyholes, and squatting down on her haunches she applied her eye to the narrow aperture.

'You've chosen the wrong room, I'm afraid, Miss Seton,' remarked an ironic voice behind her, and she got to her feet in red-faced consternation to find her employer standing watching her from the head of the stairs. She had obviously been right in assuming one of the farthest doors was his, but she felt horribly embarrassed at being discovered in such a compromising position. 'If I'd known you were interested, I'd have left the door open,' continued the mockingly derisive voice, and her lips pursed as she strove for words to erase his contemptuous assumption.

'I was looking for Anya's room, as it happens,' she declared, ignoring the sardonic twist of his mouth. 'I didn't know which room it was.'

'This is it,' he volunteered abruptly, brushing past her to open the door next to the one she had been investigating. 'But I don't really have the time right now to give you a conducted tour. However, if that really was your objective....' He gestured impatiently, and with high colour blooming in her cheeks, she stepped past him.

He had changed his clothes, that much was obvious, the rough checked shirt of the day before having given way to a slightly less coarse grey cotton. Over this he wore close-fitting jeans and a dark blue corded jacket, and as she passed him the smell of his shaving lotion was strong in her nostrils. There was something intolerably disturbing about him, a kind of sexuality that was even accentuated by the hard masculinity of his scarred face. Certainly, Joanna had never experienced the kind of reaction to a man that he aroused in her, and she decided that it was his evident indifference towards her that was causing this totally unreasonable sense of awareness.

The room into which he had invited her to look was similar to her own, in that it contained the same outdated furniture, the same unimaginative decoration, and the same bare floor. What was surprising was that here, as downstairs, there were no dolls or soft toys of any kind, and the few books that were piled beside the bed were boys' adventure stories, annuals and notebooks. The bed was unmade, obviously as Anya had climbed out if it after the punishment her father had administered the night before, and the whole room had a forlorn air, as if the state of mind of its occupant still lingered.

'Well?'

Jake was apparently waiting for her to make some comment, and forgetting her recent resentment, she made a helpless gesture. 'Doesn't she have any toys?' she asked, gazing up at him in her confusion. 'No dolls or teddies, or games of any sort? I thought I might learn something about her by discovering the things she's interested in, but there's nothing here.'

Jake's tawny eyes narrowed as they surveyed her up-turned face, and belatedly she realised that he probably thought her attitude was a deliberate attempt to attract his attention. Suspicious of her, as he was bound to be after discovering her peering through keyholes, he no doubt considered her present behaviour as typical of her frivolity, and her lids lowered in anticipation of his denunciation. But no admonishment of that sort came, even though he did draw in his breath rather harshly. Instead, his tone was expressionless when he responded:

'I wonder why you really came here, Miss Seton. Was it to help Anya? Or to satisfy my sister that I'm not impotent as well as intellectually deficient?'

Joanna's lids flicked back then, but he made no attempt to pursue this outrageous statement. As she moved out into the hall again, to escape the unavoidable intimacy he had provoked, he closed the door behind them and moved past her to the head of the stairs. Then, as if feeling obliged to make some explanation, he added:

'Since her mother's death, Anya has had no interest in girlish things; I imagine spending so much time alone with me has retarded her natural development. Perhaps you'll be successful in changing all that. Who knows?'

His eyes challenged hers again, and this time she forced herself not to appear intimidated. It was the first time she had heard his wife mentioned since Aunt Lydia had explained she had died in the same crash which had disabled her husband, and even though Joanna would have liked to pursue that topic, she shrank from the unenviable task. Evading such a personal issue, she said:

'But she has been to school, hasn't she, Mr Sheldon? And there have been other—governesses.'

He shrugged, an eloquent gesture, which seemed to dismiss her words as of no account. 'As you are aware, Miss Seton, none of them had any success with her. Schools demand too much discipline, and the women I employed to teach her seemed to regard her as being mentally subnormal.'

Joanna reserved comment. If yesterday's little fiasco was anything to go by, they might well have had reason to suppose the child backward, and she had yet to make any real contact with her.

'I really think we should be on our way,' Jake added now, starting down the stairs. 'Don't look so alarmed, Miss Seton, I don't expect miracles.' He paused halfway and looked back at her. 'But nor do I expect you to treat the job as temporary, something with which to fill your time until a more appealing proposition comes along.'

Joanna held up her head. 'I wouldn't do that, Mr Sheldon.'

'No?' He regarded her sceptically for another disturbing moment. 'Don't you think you're going to find it rather —boring here, away from the company of your friends?'

Joanna forced herself to begin the descent. 'You don't seem to want me to stay, Mr Sheldon,' she remarked quietly, calling his bluff, and without another word he turned away, his grim mouth evidence of the opinion she was confirming.

CHAPTER THREE

To Joanna's surprise, a dusty green Range Rover was parked in the cobbled yard outside the house, and Jake indicated that she should get inside. As she did so, she noticed an old man leaning on the wall beside the gates, and guessed it was Matt Coulston even before Jake threw a terse instruction to him. Then he climbed into the vehicle beside her, slammed his door, and started the engine.

'It's two miles across country,' he explained shortly, in answer to her silent enquiry, 'but it's more than twice that distance by road.'

Joanna nodded, looking out of the side window as they turned out of the gates, but she was aware of the old man's inquisitive stare as the Rover bounced up the track towards the road. It was a cool autumn morning, but the sun was quickly warming the ground, dispersing the heavy dew, and causing wisps of steam to rise from the hedgerows. It gave an added depth to the gold-swept landscape, the bare fells responding with shades of green and purple and dark sienna. She had heard of the beauty of the Lake District, but this was her first experience of it, and her antipathy towards her employer melted beneath its insidious appeal.

Through the copse, Jake stopped the Rover and got out to open the gate, but after he had driven through, Joanna pushed open her door. 'I'll close it,' she said, jumping down on to the track, and then flushed impatiently as her boot landed in a muddy pool. Still, she ignored the stains it splattered on the leg of her pants, and climbed back in again after completing her task, jaw clenched, ready to do battle if he made any sarcastic comment. He didn't, though she thought she detected a faintly ironic twist to his mouth, but she relaxed again as they reached the lane and turned towards Ravensmere.

Ravensmere was one of the smaller lakes, and the village

35

of the same name nestling at its foot was small and com-
pact, with narrow streets running down to the lakeside.
There were two hotels facing the jetty, and several cottages
advertising accommodation, and rowing boats pulled up
on the shingle, deserted now that the season was virtually
over.

Jake drove along the lake shore, skirted the village, and
after driving across a narrow hump-backed bridge, emerged
on to the road to Heronsfoot. The traffic was brisker on
this stretch of highway, connecting as it eventually did
with the main trunk road south, but presently they turned
off again on to a lane that gave way to a hikers' track, winding steadily upward until they reached a shelving plateau.
Looking across the wide expanse of the valley spread out
below them, Joanna suddenly realised that the stream at
its foot was the same stream she had seen from her bedroom
window at Ravengarth. They must have driven round in a
semi-circle, and they were now some distance up the fell
that faced north-east across the valley.

'Recognise it?' Jake said, reaching round into the back
of the vehicle and pulling out a pair of thick leather gloves.
'Here; put these on. You may have to use your hands, and
I'd hate that soft white skin to get blistered.'

Joanna pursed her lips and looked at him, but he merely
dropped the gloves into her lap and thrust open his door.
The draught of cold air his exit permitted to enter the car
made her realise how much colder it was here up on the fell,
and with a grimace she put on the gloves and joined him
outside.

'Ready?' he asked, looking down at her quizzically, and
she nodded her head.

'As I'll ever be,' she responded, holding out her hands
for his inspection. 'Aren't you afraid I'll have a major accident with these? They're far too big for me!'

'They're not for climbing,' he retorted, turning up the
collar of his jacket. 'Going up it's quite easy, but coming
down on loose shale can overbalance you. It's easier if you
squat on your hands.'

Joanna hunched her shoulders. 'If you say so,' she submitted, and with a faint arching of his brows he strode away.

They climbed a rocky incline and started up a steeper slope of scree, where tiny springs provided natural irrigation for the gorse and heather that grew on the lower slopes. A few stray sheep voiced their objections as they trotted out of their path, and a hawk hanging in the air some way above them seemed to be speculating on their possible destination.

Joanna was panting before they had climbed a hundred feet. Shopping expeditions in Oxford Street and disco dancing until the early hours were poor substitutes for real exercise, and she was glad Jake was ahead of her and therefore could not hear her laboured breathing.

About halfway up the slope, another outcrop hid the roof of a wooden hut, and Jake glanced round to see if she was with him before vaulting over the projecting face. The mist was still lingering above them, veiling the upper slopes like a shroud, and it was not difficult to imagine how easy it would be to miss their way in its blanketing folds. Struggling up behind Jake, Joanna was selfconsciously aware of her red face and trembling knees, and she guessed he was not deceived by her attempt at composure.

'This is it,' he said, and she glanced round automatically, alarmed to see how small the Range Rover looked from their superior height.

'Is—is she there?' she asked, striving to regain her breath, and he shrugged his broad shoulders before swinging down the narrow gully.

Joanna heard the dog barking as Jake approached, and presently a small figure appeared from behind the hut. Her own relief was tempered by the realisation that she was about to be properly introduced to her charge, but Jake had evidently no such misgivings. He swung the child up into his arms as the dog appeared to leap excitedly about them, and then after a brief conversation which Joanna could not hear, he turned with the child still in his arms, to climb the track back to where she was waiting.

Joanna felt an unbearable sense of disquiet as they approached. She half wished she had not succumbed to the anxiety in her employer's face and had waited back at the house, but it was too late now to have such thoughts. Instead she endeavoured to adopt an expression that was neither severe nor ingratiating, and squashed the unworthy suspicion that in Jakes's shoes she would have shown a little more anger and a little less understanding.

He set the child on her feet beside Joanna, and she looked down at her somewhat unwillingly. She could not forget their previous exchanges, in the copse and in the hall at Ravengarth, and she was quite prepared to meet aggression with aggression. But Anya's expression was almost angelically mild, and encountering wide blue eyes, innocent of all malice, Joanna wondered if she could have mistaken the child's character entirely. But how was that possible? She had been greeted with a shotgun, and no matter how obedient Anya appeared now somewhere behind that disarming gaze lurked another, less agreeable, personality.

'Anya wants to apologise, don't you?' prompted Jake now, pushing his hands into his jacket pockets, and the girl, if she really was of the feminine gender, nodded.

She was smaller than Joanna remembered, or perhaps in retrospect she had just appeared taller, and her night in the shepherd's hut had not improved her grubby appearance. The cap she had been wearing the previous afternoon was still pulled down about her ears, making the ends of her dark hair stick out almost comically at the sides. She wore an old parka, with leather patches at the elbows, jeans, and an old woollen sweater, with cuffs that hung down over her wrists. Rubber boots completed her outfit and Joanna found it amazing that a girl of her age should care so little about how she looked.

'I'm sorry, Miss Seton.' Anya was speaking now, and Joanna was amazed at the attractiveness of her voice after the coarse language she had used the day before. 'It was silly, running off like that. It didn't solve anything.'

Joanna digested these words rather doubtfully. There was something wrong here. She didn't know why she felt so sure, but she did. Last night Anya had been slapped and put to bed after behaving quite appallingly. She had sobbed and screamed, and shown every indication of anger and resentment, even to the extent of actually running away. Now she was apologising, saying she was sorry, that she had been silly, that it hadn't *solved* anything. Solve was a curious word to use. Finding any kind of solution in the circumstances had an ominous ring to it, and Joanna looked rather blankly at her employer, wondering if he had detected anything unusual about his daughter's behaviour. But he apparently had not. He was obviously waiting for her to make the next move, and with a grimace she said:

'You didn't expect me to leave, did you, Anya? I'm not that easily deterred. Your father and I only want what's best for you, and I'm sure you're not going to disappoint us.'

Joanna didn't quite know why she used that particular approach, or indeed why she should attempt to antagonise the child with her first words. She was aware that Jake was looking at her in some irritation, and evidently he would have preferred a more conciliatory tone, but Joanna had already sensed that with Anya, one had to stay one jump ahead. Even so, she felt a certain ripple of apprehension slide along her spine as she glimpsed the sudden anger that filled the child's eyes, and guessed that her deliberate linking of herself and Anya's father had aroused that instinctive response. So she was right, she thought, without any of the exhilaration she should have been feeling. Anya was only bluffing, but what kind of an advantage did that give her?

'I think Anya is beginning to realise that these stupid, childish pranks are just a waste of time,' Jake pronounced heavily, his breath vaporising in the chilly air. 'She's growing up. She has to learn to take responsibility for her actions. And now I suggest we go back to the car. Anya needs some hot food and a change of clothes, and then perhaps we can start behaving like civilised people.'

Joanna was glad of the leather gloves going down the hillside again. She was not used to the steepness of the slope, and she soon learned the advantages of squatting down on her heels and controlling her slide with her hands. Anya, of course, had no such fears. She and the dog, Binzer, bounded down the loose shale with complete confidence, and even Jake kept his balance without apparent effort. It was a little annoying for Joanna to have to complete her descent under Anya's intent appraisal, but she managed to get to her feet near the bottom and meet the girl's gaze with bland enquiry, hoping the trembling uncertainty of her knees could not be detected.

There was no argument about who should sit where in the Range Rover. Jake ordered Anya and the dog into the back, and Joanna got into the seat beside him with some relief. It had been quite an exhausting trip, one way and another, and she slumped rather wearily against the upholstery as he started the engine. The journey back to Ravengarth was completed almost in silence, but Joanna was aware all the way of the physical presence of Anya's knees digging into her back, and the not-so-physical awareness of her resentful gaze boring into the back of her head.

As they neared the house, however, Joanna remembered she was still wearing the gloves he had given her, and tugging them off her now sweating palms she dropped them on to the shelf in front of her.

'Thank you,' she murmured, glancing sideways at her employer, and a vaguely amused quirk tilted his eyebrow.

'I saw you made use of them,' he said, with a wry grimace. 'You're no fell-runner, I think.'

'I'm not the outdoor type,' retorted Joanna shortly, forgetting for a moment that they had an audience, and the amusement deepened in his eyes.

'That's the truth,' he confirmed, turning off the lane on to the track for Ravengarth, and she was dismayed to find she wanted to laugh. It had been such a curious morning, and it wasn't half over yet, and she could picture her friends' reaction if she confessed to them that she had been climbing grubby hillsides before nine o'clock and sliding down them again on the seat of her pants.

'You're supposed to run down the shale,' said a clear scornful voice behind them, that completely dissipated the humour of the situation. 'That's how you keep your balance. Only dogs and babies slide on their *bottoms*!'

'Thank you, Anya, that will do.'

Jake's curt remonstrance was immediate, and Joanna wondered why the girl had so quickly forgotten the role she had intended to play. If she imagined she could delude her father into thinking she was a reformed character one minute, and then revert to her objectionable self the next, she was very much mistaken.

However, Anya was already restoring her image. 'I'm sorry, Daddy,' she was saying, adopting a wounded tone. 'I didn't mean to be rude. But it's true, isn't it? You are supposed to run down the shale. It's not half as dangerous as it sounds.'

'Experts run down the shale, Anya, inexperienced climbers don't,' Jake retorted, pulling up at the gate that gave on to the copse and pushing open his door. 'No one could call Miss Seton an experienced climber, and I expect you to show a little more respect.'

He went to open the gate, and Joanna waited resignedly for the retaliation she was sure would come. She wasn't disappointed. Anya only waited until the door had closed behind her father before saying in a low, venomous voice:

'Don't think I'm going to let you stay here, just because you think you've won the first round! I can get rid of you any time I like, and I will!'

Joanna listened, but as she did so her own anger flared, and she turned on the child without consideration for her age or her inexperience. 'Now you listen to me, you little hellcat,' she spat furiously, 'no one, but no one, speaks to me like that! Just who do you think you are? Dressed like a scarecrow, with brains to match! Do you think I want to teach you? Do you think I want to stay here in this hole, living in a house that pigs would find offensive? You're a joke, do you know that? A living, breathing *joke*, and if it was up to me, you wouldn't be able to slide down shale on your bottom! You wouldn't even be able to sit on it!'

Anya shrank back in her seat as she spoke, and if Joanna had been less incensed, she would have seen much sooner how her outburst was draining all the colour out of the child's cheeks. As it was, she had barely registered the fact before another angry voice broke into her tirade.

'What in God's name do you think you're doing?' Jake had jerked open his door and was climbing savagely back into the Rover. He glared incredulously at Joanna before turning to look at his daughter, and then shook his head disbelievingly as she took advantage of the situation and burst instantly into tears. 'Heavens above, I get out of the car for two minutes to open the gate, and you take leave of your senses! If this is your idea of gaining a child's confidence, I suggest you pack your bags right away. This isn't Dothegirls Hall, Miss Seton, and I do not condone adults acting like children, whatever the provocation!'

Joanna pressed her lips mutinously together, hunching her shoulders against the acidity of his stare. What was the point of staying here, as he said? Anya didn't want to learn; she didn't even want to behave civilly. They were all just wasting their time trying to change her. What she needed was a keeper, not a governess, and Joanna simply hadn't the patience to humour her.

'She said our house was a pigsty,' Anya sniffed indignantly, and Joanna was forced to defend herself when Jake demanded if this was so.

'It's true,' she declared, holding up her head. 'Your— your housekeeper doesn't know how to keep house, and the food she serves is appalling. I don't know what you pay her, but whatever it is, it's too much!'

Jake was gazing at her as if he couldn't believe what he was hearing, and Joanna acknowledged to herself that the situation was unique. He had obviously never had to rebuke the governess before, but if he expected her to apologise and beg to be kept on, he was very much mistaken. It might be pigheaded, it might be a case of cutting off her nose to spite her face; but she was not some mealy-mouthed spinster, willing to suffer any kind of humiliation in order to keep her position. No eleven-year-old was going to make a fool of her, and if it meant her having to take a job in a shop or a factory, then so be it. Anything was better than struggling to save her self-respect with this little savage. In consequence, she was able to meet Jake's steel-hard eyes with almost insolent indifference, and sensed that he had never been so near to striking a woman before.

Without another word he swung round in his seat, slammed his door, and drove through the gateway. Then, standing on his brakes so that she was almost projected through the windscreen, he got out to close the gate again, leaving his door open this time so that he could hear any exchange there might be. But Anya was either too clever, or too distressed, to be caught that way. She continued to sniff rather plaintively in the back of the vehicle, not responding to Binzer's mournful whining, or blowing her nose as Joanna could have wished.

When Jake climbed in again, Joanna avoided his gaze, staring rather disconsolately out of the window. She remembered the anticipation she had felt on the outward journey, and her mouth turned down rather cynically at the corners. There should be a union for governesses, she decided, pursing her lips half indignantly. Unfair dismissal, that was what she was being given, and just because she had no desire to stay, was no reason to force her to leave. All right, so she had spoken her mind—wasn't that better than pretending a liking for the girl she didn't feel? At least she and Anya understood one another now, even if the next female to be employed was bound to suffer the consequences of her outburst.

She sighed, casting a surreptitious look in her employer's direction. His profile, set against the shadows of the copse, was hard and unyielding, yet she suddenly knew an illogical feeling of sympathy for him. It couldn't be easy, trying to bring up a rebellious child like Anya single-handed, particularly in his personal circumstances. Losing his wife like that, losing his career; she and her mother had thought the world had come to an end when her father had died and left them without any money. *Money!* Money couldn't solve Jake Sheldon's problems. They were much more complex than that, and her conscience pricked her at the suspicion that she had perhaps added to them.

Jake parked the Range Rover in the yard and climbed out rather aggressively, Joanna thought. 'Indoors, bath, and hair washed,' he ordered the still sniffing Anya, and after she had departed trailing the confused Binzer, he turned back to Joanna.

'I want to see you in the library in five minutes,' he told her curtly, before striding away towards the stables. 'Please don't keep me waiting.'

Joanna stared after him in some amazement, and then with a helpless shrug she thrust open her door. She almost stood on a chicken as she put her foot to the ground, and it ran squawking away as she drew a steadying breath. Well, he wanted to give her her notice, didn't he? she argued with herself, as she picked her way towards the house, and then felt a wave of weariness sweep over her as she saw Mrs Harris waiting at the door. She could tell from the housekeeper's face that Anya had not wasted any time in relating her comments, and she squared her shoulders a little defiantly to bolster her fast-fading confidence.

'I want a word with you—*miss*!' Mrs Harris declared, as she approached, and for a minute Joanna thought she wasn't going to let her into the house. But although she was slim, she was quite strong, and evidently the housekeeper decided her grievances fell short of physical violence.

Joanna brushed past her into the hall of the house, her upbringing deterring her from conducting any kind of argument outdoors, and Mrs Harris had no choice but to follow her into the library.

'What's all this you've been saying about my housekeeping?' she demanded, as soon as Joanna had crossed the threshold. 'What right have you to make remarks about how I looks after this place? I'll have you know, I've been here nigh on thirty years, and no one's ever complained before.'

'Really?' Joanna didn't want to get involved in this. It was no business of hers if she was leaving. But she could hardly believe that she was the first to notice the deplorable state of the place.

'Yes, really,' Mrs Harris continued aggressively. 'There was no complaints when Mr Fawcett was alive, and since he's gone and Mr Sheldon's took over, he's never said he wasn't satisfied with my work.'

'Perhaps Mr Sheldon, being a man, doesn't care about such things,' put in Joanna carefully, and Mrs Harris let out an indignant howl.

'You cheeky young madam, coming here with your hoity-toity ways, putting on airs and graces, pretending you're something you're not! Why, Mrs Hunter herself told us you and your mother was practically penniless since that father of yours gambled all his money away, and you were forced to look for work to support the two of you!'

Joanna's cheeks burned. What had Aunt Lydia told Jake Sheldon's sister? How had she phrased the offer of her goddaughter's services to educate her niece? And how had Marcia Hunter described her to her brother, that his house-keeper should speak so disparagingly of it?

'My personal affairs are no concern of yours, Mrs Harris,' she said now, trying desperately to maintain her detachment. If she once resorted to a slanging match with the woman, she would lose all semblance of self-respect, and that was something she must retain at all costs.

'Personal affairs!' sneered Mrs Harris scornfully. 'Your affairs aren't personal. It was in all the papers—how your father broke his neck trying to jump a fence when he was drunk——'

'He wasn't drunk,' denied Joanna hotly, unable to stay silent on that score. 'The horse bolted——'

'So you say.'

'It's the truth!'

Mrs Harris obviously didn't believe her, but she changed her tactics. 'You soon found out who your friends was, though, didn't you?' she taunted. 'All them posh ways of yours count for nothing when you've got no money, do they? And you come here, criticising me! I don't know how you have the nerve! Saying I keep a dirty house—complaining about my cooking—telling Mr Sheldon that the food is appalling——'

'It is,' asserted a hard masculine voice behind them, and their employer came impatiently into the room, applying the flame of the slim gold lighter in his hand to the narrow cigar between his teeth. 'You're fired, Mrs Harris. I should have done it long ago, but I'm afraid I've allowed everything to slide since—since coming here. I intend to rectify that. And your dismissal is long overdue.'

Joanna didn't know which one of them was the most astounded, herself or Mrs Harris. The last thing she had expected was that he might actually act on what she had said, and in spite of her aversion for the housekeeper's slovenly ways, she couldn't help but sympathise with such an abrupt expulsion.

Mrs Harris's mouth was opening and shutting like a goldfish, and for a couple of minutes she could say nothing at all. But then she found her tongue, and recriminations spilled from it with vituperative force.

'You can't do this, Mr Sheldon!' she cried, at first appealing to his better nature. 'I've been here at Ravengarth since I was a girl. Why, I came here just after the war, when Mrs Fawcett had her first baby, and I've been here ever since.'

'Perhaps you should retire, Mrs Harris.' Jake's voice was flat as he strode round the desk and stood with arms folded, waiting for her to leave. With the cigar between his teeth, a strand of the straight dark hair lying smoothly across his forehead, his scarred face possessed a harsh and brooding fascination, and Joanna had to drag her shocked gaze away before he noticed her involuntary appraisal.

The housekeeper spent a few more minutes extolling the way she had struggled to care for Ravengarth single-handed, how she was not as young as she used to be, and that she had never complained, but when she saw she was making no headway she resorted to cruder methods.

'Don't think I can't see what's going on here,' she declared, nodding unpleasantly. 'I can see the way the wind's blowing. You want me out of the way, so's you and 'er,' she flicked a thumb in Joanna's direction, 'won't have no supervision. That's it, isn't it? As soon as I saw her I knew. You think with me out of the way you'll have a clear field. No one to spy on you, only a child, and 'er half wild as it is.' She sniffed expressively. 'Well, I'd not stand for that, if I was you, Miss Seton!' *What had happend to improve her opinion of her suddenly?* Joanna wondered in amazement. 'He's got a foul temper, he has. Specially when the weather's cold, and them scars start playing him up——'

'Mrs Harris——'

'Get out, Mrs Harris!'

Joanna's horrified exclamation was overidden by Jake's angry response. As he came round the desk, his manner was almost threatening and the housekeeper took a nervous backward step as she made her final attempt to dissuade him.

'You'll not get anyone else to come here and work for you,' she warned shrilly. 'And you needn't expect that young madam to help you. She's leaving, she is—Anya told me. And in any case, you wouldn't expect the likes of 'er to go dirtying 'er hands in honest labour. Too stuck-up for that, she is, let me tell you!'

'Out,' said Jake uncompromisingly. 'Pack your belongings at once, and I'll drive you to your sister's at Lancaster. And if I hear that you've been spreading any gossip about me or Miss Seton, I'll make sure the authorities hear about it. A case for slander is not that difficult to prove, not when there are plenty of people hereabouts who remember the old days. Do I make myself understood?'

Mrs Harris stared at him a little apprehensively now, but she was not completely convinced. 'What do you mean —the old days?' she protested indignantly. 'I've always done my work to the best of my ability, and you can't prove otherwise. Why, Mrs Fawcett depended on me, she did——'

'That's not what I've heard,' Jake informed her coldly. 'In fact, I'd go so far as to say that Mrs Fawcett would have liked to get rid of you herself, only she was too ill at the time.'

'That's—that's libel——'

'If it wasn't true, the word is slander, as I've just explained,' Jake retorted bleakly. 'However, as I have every reason to believe it is true, and as I'm not likely to repeat it beyond these walls, I don't see what you can do about it.'

Mrs Harris's mouth pursed. 'Who's been saying such things? It's that Matt Coulston, isn't it?'

Jake sighed then, and shook his head. 'You know Matt, Mrs Harris,' he replied wearily. 'He's not the type to gossip about anyone.'

'I should think not! Not when he's little more than a——'

'That will do, Mrs Harris. I should go before you say something you regret.'

Her lip jutted. 'You're not frightening me!'

'Am I not?'

The woman's thin face suffused with colour. 'You'll regret this, just see if you don't. There's no decent person would put up with that besom upstairs——'

But this time she had gone too far, and she scuttled quickly out of the door as he approached her with clenched fists.

It took Jake a few minutes to recover his composure after this exchange, and Joanna turned awkwardly away, shifting from one foot to the other. She didn't honestly know what to expect after his unexpected dismissal of the housekeeper, and she wondered if he intended to drop her at Penrith station on his way to Lancaster. It would certainly be a clean sweep if he did, but what would happen to Anya then? Curiously enough, the thought disturbed her, and she squashed the awareness that it was Anya's father who aroused these feelings of responsibility inside her.

Presently he came back to the desk again, and she chanced a brief glance up at his bleak face as he positioned himself behind it. She didn't know why the weariness of his expression disturbed her, but it did, and she wished she had not spoken so recklessly earlier.

'Sit down,' he said, and in some relief she did as he asked. At least she was being offered the chance to take her punishment sitting down, she thought dejectedly, wondering what had happened to the anger that had given her such confidence in the car.

Jake took a long pull at his cigar, and then seated himself in the worn chair opposite, thick black lashes veiling the expression in his eyes as he shifted the papers on the desk, as if like herself he was searching for a suitable opening. Then, as if coming to a decision, he lifted his head and said:

'I have to ask you if you'll do something for me.'

His words were so unlike anything she had anticipated that for a moment she didn't make any response, but when his mouth assumed a downward slant, she licked her lips and asked: 'What is it?' in faintly apprehensive tones.

He lay back in his chair then, surveying her through the haze of cigar smoke he had emitted. Like that, relaxed, his expression vaguely speculative, Joanna could quite see why women had found him so attractive, and Mrs Harris's accusations did not seem quite so outrageous suddenly.

But his next words dispelled any illusions she might have entertained. 'As you heard, I have to take Mrs Harris to Lancaster. I'm asking you to remain at Ravengarth and take charge of Anya until I return.'

Joanna suppressed the disappointment his words engendered. 'Why can't you take her with you?' she exclaimed, in the heat of the implied rejection, and immediately he came upright in his chair.

'Because I would prefer Anya not to have to listen to any more of the woman's lies,' he retorted coldly. 'I realise I'm asking this favour from a position of weakness, but if you could oblige me in this way, I'm quite prepared to see you don't suffer by it.'

Joanna's lips pursed. 'You'll pay me, you mean?'

'I'll pay you,' he agreed dourly. 'Is it a deal?'

Joanna sighed. 'I don't know ...'

'Oh, not more indecision, Miss Seton! Either you will or you won't. It's as simple as that. I promise you, whatever Mrs Harris says, I have no ulterior designs on your virtue.'

Joanna flushed. 'I didn't expect you had, Mr Sheldon.'

'Good. So we understand one another.'

'Do we?'

He expelled his breath wearily. 'What's that supposed to mean? I'm sorry, I'm out of touch with these double-edged conversations.'

Joanna hesitated. 'Are you dismissing me, Mr Sheldon?'

'Am I dismissing you?' He stared at her blankly. 'Forgive me, but I understood it was your intention to leave!'

Joanna held up her head. 'It was you who said this wasn't a Dickensian establishment! It was you who suggested I should pack my bags!'

He propped one elbow on the desk and rested his head on his hand. 'Let's get this straight, shall we? You were arguing with Anya, like a pair of cats in a barn. What the hell was I supposed to say?'

Joanna blinked. 'But what about Mrs Harris? What I said about her? I mean, you've fired her, but ... well ...'

He lifted his head, and let his arm fall indifferently on to the desk. 'Do I take it she was being presumptuous? That you actually want to *stay*?'

Joanna hunched her shoulders, moving her head a trifle bewilderedly, aware that her hair had come loose from its knot in places, and was falling about her ears in silken disorder. But she had other things to worry about at the moment, not least her own confusion at this unexpected reprieve.

'I thought you wanted me to leave,' she said at last, unwilling to commit herself, and he thrust back his chair and got to his feet.

'Look, Miss Seton,' he said heavily, 'I employed you to teach Anya, and for no other reason. But I also accept that since you came here the situation has been anything but stable. Consequently I'm prepared to overlook any outburst which may or may not have been precipitated by tension. However, I should point out that as I now no longer have a housekeeper, it may not be in your best interests to remain. I shall certainly endeavour to find a replacement, but I have to tell you that the women in the village have already refused to work here.'

Joanna looked up at him. 'Why?'

His expression hardened, the ridges of scar tissue standing out clearly against his dark skin. 'Can't you guess?' he demanded harshly, long fingers probing the roughened flesh. 'Who would want to face *this* across the breakfast table every morning, unless you had no alternative?'

Joanna stood up. 'That's nonsense,' she declared fiercely. 'You've lived with it for too long, Mr Sheldon. Believe me, it's not half as bad as you imagine it to be. In fact——'

'Spare me the platitudes, Miss Seton. I've heard them all before.'

'But——'

'And besides, there are other reasons why the villagers wouldn't want to work at Ravengarth. It's generally believed in the village that I'm a little—eccentric, to say the least, and Anya's behaviour doesn't help. They know I couldn't cope with my work after the accident, and they assume that means—slightly retarded, not quite *compos mentis*.'

'But that's ludicrous!' exclaimed Joanna incredulously, and he moved his shoulders in a dismissing gesture.

'How do you know? How can you be so sure? Perhaps they're right. Perhaps I am a little—insane. God knows, I have reason to be, after living this kind of existence for the past two years.'

Joanna bent her head. 'Do you want me to stay?' she asked quietly. 'Aren't you afraid I might—disrupt your tranquillity?'

'Tranquillity?' He made a disbelieving sound. 'What tranquillity? I don't know what tranquillity is, Miss Seton.' He paused. 'But in answer to your question—yes, I want you to stay. Your—unusual approach may be exactly what's needed to get through to Anya. Either way, it can be no harm for her to be given a taste of her own medicine for a change, providing you understand you are answerable to me in the final analysis.'

Joanna lifted her head. 'Very well.'

'Good.'

The tawny eyes held hers for a long moment, but although she was disturbed by that probing gaze, she could tell from his expression that his mind was already moving ahead to other things. Yet, for all that, when he looked away she felt a sense almost of fatigue, and she followed him out of the room with the uneasy suspicion that she might live to regret ever coming here.

CHAPTER FOUR

JAKE left soon after eleven, with a sober-faced Mrs Harris beside him in the Range Rover. It had to be a sad day for the woman, thought Joanna, guiltily aware of her own part in her dismissal, but as she surveyed the empty hall, she had to concede that the decision had been long overdue. Maybe when Mrs Fawcett had been alive, she had worked satisfactorily under her supervision, but since that lady's death it seemed Mrs Harris had made little effort in any direction.

Realising that someone would have to take temporary charge of the household, Joanna walked down the passage in search of the kitchen. She found the stone-flagged room at the back of the house, overlooking a vegetable garden, just as Mrs Harris had left it, with the remains of the morning's breakfast still clinging to the plates in the sink. It was a daunting sight, particularly to someone with Joanna's limited knowledge of domestic affairs, but in spite of the morning's upheavals she found she was hungry, and somehow she would have to produce a meal that she and Anya could share.

She knew Jake had spoken to his daughter before he left, but she didn't know what he had told her. He merely advised Joanna that Anya was drying her hair, and that she would come downstairs when she was finished.

The kitchen itself was no miracle of modern technology. There was a white sink and a wooden draining board, an electric cooker that had probably been there since Mrs Fawcett's time, and a twin-tub electric washing machine, presently overflowing with dirty linen. There was an ancient refrigerator, whose freezing compartment was not even enclosed, and several fitted cupboards to line the walls. Meals were apparently taken on the wooden table that occupied the middle of the floor, and the room was heated by a blackened Aga boiler that probably heated the water and those elderly radiators upstairs. Luckily the boiler was going; Mrs Harris obviously liked her comforts, thought Joanna ruefully, remembering the chilly atmosphere of the rest of the house, but at least it meant that there was plenty of hot water, and she soon had the sink full of soapy suds.

With the dishes done, she turned attention to more immediate matters, like what food there was in the house, and where it was kept. She discovered a cool larder that opened off the kitchen, whose stone shelves would probably keep butter and milk as fresh as in the fridge, but at present there were only tinned foods stacked in rows, and half a loaf of stale bread lying on a wooden board.

There were plenty of eggs, she saw, probably gathered from the hens she had seen in the yard, but from the window the vegetable garden looked bare of any produce, and she guessed that what had been grown had been used.

She was studying the label on the back of a can of mixed vegetables when there was a tapping at the back door. Immediately, her thoughts sprang to the awareness that she was alone in the house, apart from the child, and she peered anxiously through the window, trying to see who it was before she actually opened the door.

'Lily? Are you there, Lily?'

Joanna was still struggling to discover who it was, when the door opened behind her, and she swung round in alarm as a man came into the kitchen. His sharp eyes soon found her shrinking against the draining board, and while he exhibited almost as much surprise at finding her there, Joanna was able to identify him. He was the old man who had been leaning on the wall that morning, watching her and Jake depart in search of Anya. Matt Coulston; or at least that was her assumption, and obviously he didn't know yet that Mrs Harris had gone.

Recovering herself quickly, Joanna moved away from the sink. 'You're Mr Coulston, aren't you?' she asked, trying to keep her tone light and friendly. 'I'm afraid if you're looking for Mrs Harris, she's not here.'

'Not here?' he echoed, his greying brows beetling above

a hooked nose. 'What do you mean, she's not here? Where is she? Where's she gone?'

'She's left,' said Joanna firmly, waiting slightly apprehensively for his reaction. 'Mr—er—Mr Sheldon fired her. They left about half an hour ago.'

'Well, I'm damned!' The old man slapped his thigh with unexpected enthusiasm. 'Jake's done it at last! He's got rid of the old besom. I didn't think he had it in him.'

Joanna didn't know how to answer this, so instead she said: 'Is there something I can do for you, Mr Coulston? Until Mr Sheldon gets back, I'm looking after the place.'

'Oh, you are, are you?' This seemed to amuse him. 'Then you'll be wanting this, won't you? Seeing as how *you're* looking after things!' and he swung the hand that had been hanging by his side as he spoke, and deposited a dead chicken on the kitchen table. Joanna had never seen anything so repulsive before. The chickens she had cooked had all been plucked and ready for the table, whereas this creature was barely cold, and still covered in its feathery coat.

'Did—did Mrs Harris ask for this, Mr Coulston?' she got out eventually, and he nodded.

'Wanted it for supper this evening,' he declared, pushing the limp body across to her. 'That's Gloria, that is. One of my best layers, in her time. Getting lazy, she was. Must be getting old, Miss ... er ... Anyway, she's done for now. Comes to all of us eventually, doesn't it?'

Joanna licked her dry lips. 'I've never plucked a chicken before,' she murmured, half to herself. Then: 'Well— thank you, Mr Coulston. I—er—I'll do what I can.'

His dark eyes narrowed as he looked at her, and then, almost inconsequently, he said: 'I thought you came here to governess that young rip Anya. I didn't know you was a housekeeper.'

'I'm not.' Joanna sighed, realising he probably deserved an explanation. 'I am here to teach Anya. But until Mr Sheldon gets someone else ...'

'I see,' the old man nodded. 'And what's a young lassie like you doing in a place like this? From London, ain't you?

Don't the young fellers down there have any eyes?'

Joanna smiled at that. 'That's a nice compliment, Mr Coulston, but I'm not that keen to get married. Besides, no one asked me.'

'No?' He looked sceptical, and she gave a soft laugh.

'Well, no one I wanted to accept,' she conceded, and he chuckled in response.

'So you're going to try and teach some manners to young Anya?'

'That is my intention.'

He grimaced. 'Well, the best of luck! She's not going to be an easy target. Run wild for too long, she has, with only a couple of helpless old biddies to chase after her.'

Joanna laughed again—she couldn't help it. It didn't seem to matter that he was saying virtually the same thing as Mrs Harris had told her. It was the way he said them that mattered, and she sensed that unlike the housekeeper, he had some affection for the girl.

'And your name's Miss—what?' he asked gruffly. 'Can't go on saying you-know-who all the time, can I?'

'It's Seton, actually,' replied Joanna easily. 'Joanna Seton. How do you do, Mr Coulston?'

'The name's Matt,' he told her, moving towards the door again. 'No need for all that formal stuff.' He looked down at the chicken and then after a moment picked it up again. 'And I'll pluck old Gloria for you, and clean her out. Seeing as how you got shot of old Mother Harris.'

'But I didn't,' protested Joanna, and found she was speaking to a closed door.

She had decided she would have to walk to the village that afternoon for some bread and flour, and was busily whipping up some eggs for lunch, when Anya came into the room. It was the first time Joanna had seen her with her face clean, and the transformation was quite amazing. With her hair decently cut, and wearing something other than those disreputable jeans, she would look quite attractive, Joanna reflected thoughtfully; the contrast of blue eyes—her mother's?—and dark hair—her father's—could be quite a combination.

Nevertheless, the improvement in her appearance did not make Joanna less wary of her. On the contrary, she was actively prepared for a resumption of hostilities, and Anya's first words did nothing to allay her suspicions.

'Where's Mrs Harris?' she asked, standing just inside the door from the hall. 'This is Mrs Harris's kitchen, not yours. You shouldn't be in here.'

Joanna sighed, and put down the bowl of eggs she had been beating. 'I'm sure your father told you, Mrs Harris has left,' she said carefully. 'Now, do you want an omelette for your lunch, or will you get what you want yourself?'

'So long as you're making them, I'll have an omelette,' the girl declared insolently, moving further into the room and straddling a chair at the table. 'Daddy didn't tell me you were going to be the new housekeeper. Why do we have to have you? I want Mrs Harris.'

Joanna steeled herself not to respond as Anya wanted her to do. She would enjoy telling her father how Miss Seton had abused her while he was away, and while Joanna felt reasonably sure that he was not duped by his daughter's behaviour, nevertheless she knew he would not approve of her resorting to a child's methods of retaliation a second time.

Instead she smiled sweetly and said: 'You really are the most obnoxious child, Antonia. And I like you no more than you like me. But we're going to get along together, one way or the other, and you might as well get used to the fact.'

'My name's Anya,' snapped the girl angrily, springing to her feet. 'And I'll never get along with you. The others were bad enough, but you're worse. *They* never got Daddy to get rid of Mrs Harris, and *they* never made eyes at him every chance they got!'

Joanna gasped—she couldn't help it. The last thing she had done was make eyes at Jake Sheldon, and for a minute she felt so angry she could have slapped Anya's face.

It took all her self-control to pick up the bowl of eggs again and expunge her frustration on them as she answered: 'I did not ask your father to dismiss Mrs Harris, and as

for being interested in him, that's ludicrous! I hardly know
him, and besides, he's not my type.'

'Because of his face?'

Anya's question was unexpectedly anxious, and Joanna
quickly shook her head. 'Of course not. That has nothing
to do with it.'

'Doesn't it?' Anya sounded disbelieving now. 'He says
no woman would want to look at a gargoyle every day of
her life.'

Joanna sighed, reluctantly stirred by the child's involuntary confidence. 'Your father is far too sensitive about his
appearance,' she said firmly. 'You don't mind looking at
him, do you?'

'Me?' Anya sat down again almost unthinkingly. 'Of
course not! I love him. And I don't care how he looks.'

'There you are, then.' Joanna lifted a heavy frying pan
down from a shelf and put it on the top of the cooker.
'When you love someone, you don't judge them on appearance. You care for them for who they are, what they are,
what they mean to you.'

Anya was silent for a few minutes, and Joanna added fat
to the pan with a feeling almost of disbelief. Who would
have believed that only seconds ago she would have been
saying such things to this little termagant, who even now
was probably thinking of some new mischief to perform.

The omelettes didn't take long to cook, and she heated
the tin of mixed vegetables at the same time. It wasn't
really a satisfying meal to give a hungry eleven-year-old,
she thought ruefully, but until she could get to the shops
and stock up on some essential foods, it would have to do.

Anya tucked into her omelette with gusto, and remembering that she had had nothing since the night before,
Joanna wasn't altogether surprised. On impulse she opened
a can of sliced peaches to give her for dessert, and watched
the whole lot disappear while she enjoyed a decent cup of
instant coffee.

When the meal was over, Anya rose from the table at
once, but Joanna was not about to let her get away like that.
'You can help me with the dishes,' she said briskly, pushing

back her chair. 'And then you can show me the way to the village.'

Anya's protests at the former request were stifled by her curiosity at the latter. 'Why do you want to know the way to the village?' she exclaimed, looking suspicious. 'You won't be welcome there. Ravensmere people don't like us. They think we're—peculiar.' A thought seemed to occur to her at this, and she hunched her shoulders in a menacing pose. 'Perhaps we are.'

'I expect even monsters have to eat sometimes,' responded Joanna matter-of-factly, carrying their dirty dishes to the sink. 'I want to do some shopping, that's all. I doubt if anyone will refuse my money.'

Anya frowned. 'You can't go shopping in Ravensmere —we never do. Daddy always takes Mrs Harris into Penrith, and she goes to the supermarket there.'

'Well, for once it won't matter,' Joanna retorted blandly. 'Hurry up, bring those plates here. I want to get down to the village and back again before your father gets home.'

Anya looked as though she was going to argue and then thought better of it, shrugging her thin shoulders as she carried the crockery to the sink. If only she could get through to her, thought Joanna hopefully. How much simpler her task would be!

Matt returned with the plucked chicken as she was putting the clean dishes away, and Joanna smiled at him gratefully as he put the bird on the table. 'It really was kind of you,' she murmured, wishing there was some way that she could repay him, but he only winked at her before turning his attention to the child.

'And don't you go giving Miss Seton a lot of bother, young 'un,' he declared, taking her pointed chin in his gnarled hand and tipping her face up to his. 'About time someone took you in hand, it is, and I'm putting my money on Miss Seton to be the one to do it.'

'Oh, are you?'

Anya jerked her chin away, her mouth assuming a rebellious curve, and Joanna couldn't help wishing he had not made such a statement. It was tantamount to provocation, and Anya was not likely to let it go unchallenged.

'What time did Jake say he'd be back, Miss Seton?' Matt continued, now turning to Joanna, and with one eye on Anya, she shrugged her slim shoulders.

'He didn't. But he was taking Mrs Harris to her sister's in Lancaster, so perhaps you'd know how long that would take.'

Matt tugged thoughtfully at his chin. 'Left about eleven o'clock, you said, didn't you? Should be there soon after one. I reckon he might be back before four.' He frowned. 'Seems like we might as well leave those ditches till to-morrow.'

Joanna hesitated. 'You mean—you and Mr Sheldon were going to—work on these ditches together?'

'That's what I said.'

Joanna nodded, uneasily remembering what had happened the day before. What would Jake have said in these circumstances? Was Matt's weakness for the bottle likely to rear its ugly head again in his employer's absence?

Taking an impulsive decision, she said: 'The—er—the garden out back seems a bit neglected. If you've got nothing else to do, Mr Coulston, perhaps you could start digging it over. I'm not absolutely sure about these things, but isn't it possible to sow crops now that will provide early vegetables in the spring?'

Anya's indignant expression changed to one of malicious anticipation at Joanna's suggestion. 'Yes, why don't you dig the garden over, Matt?' she taunted impudently. 'Miss Seton's very good at finding jobs for everybody but herself.'

'That's not true, Anya!'

Joanna spoke defensively, and then quickly turned her irritation to a smile as she encountered Matt's puzzled features. The last thing she wanted to do was antagonise the one person who had shown her a little understanding since she came here, and she hoped her hasty words had not jeopardised their friendship.

'I only thought ...' she began awkwardly, and then

breathed a sigh of relief when she saw his eyes were twinkling.

'I fancy Jake's been telling you about those attacks I have from time to time, Miss Seton,' he said, scratching his head through the thinning threads of his hair. 'Seems like you're worried that the devil himself will take charge of these idle hands.'

'Mr Coulston, honestly——'

'The name's Matt, and don't you forget it. And if you want the kitchen garden digging over, then I'll be happy to do it for you.' He waggled a finger at Anya as he spoke. 'And don't you go trying to get me and Miss Seton at odds with one another, just because you don't want to learn how to behave yourself.'

Anya's lips compressed into a mutinous line. 'I know how to behave myself,' she declared hotly. 'And you're a fine one to talk about behaviour! I know where you were last night.'

'Anya!'

Joanna was horrified, but Matt only held up his hand. 'She doesn't mean any harm,' he said, his eyes on the girl's flushed face. 'She's like a hare, trapped in the woods. Try as it might, it can't get free, and when someone happens along and tries to release it, it claws and scratches and bites without realising someone's trying to help it.'

'Don't tell me your tales, Matt Coulston,' Anya retorted with a grimace. 'I don't need any help, if that's what you're trying to say. I know everything I need to know to live here, and that's all that matters.'

'And what happens when your daddy goes back to London?' enquired Matt patiently. 'Do you think he wants his daughter behaving like a little savage?'

'Daddy's not going back to London,' declared Anya, but there was a note of anxiety in her tones that she could not quite disguise. 'He—he wouldn't be happy there. He said so. And in any case, it's nothing to do with you, so there!'

She threw herself out of the room without another word, and Joanna breathed a sigh of resignation. Anya would probably disappear again now, and her hopes of finding a short cut to the village seemed doomed to failure.

Then a thought suddenly struck her. 'Mr Coulston—Matt!'

He halted in the process of going out the door. 'Yes?'

'Could I walk to the village from here? I mean, without going round by the road? It must be about three miles that way. I wondered if there was a short cut.'

Matt frowned, and looked as if he was about to ask why she wanted to go to Ravensmere. Then he seemed to think better of it, and shrugging his slightly-stooped shoulders, he said: 'You can walk down to the stream and follow the path that takes you to Piper's Bridge, but I wouldn't advise it. With all this rain we've been having, the path's flooded in places, and you could find your feet sliding into the water.'

'Oh, dear!' Joanna grimaced.

'There is the other way,' he added doubtfully. 'Young Anya could show it to you. It's a bit more complicated to describe, you see. It means going round through the copse, over Trevor's field, and down into the village by the lane from the farm.'

Joanna's face brightened. 'That sounds more interesting. I'm sure I could find it, Matt, if you just told me exactly how to reach this farm track.'

It was a little complicated, remembering the path she had to take through the wood, and which field skirted the farm buildings, but when she left the kitchen to go up to her room to get ready she felt reasonably confident of her route. She washed her face and hands, applied a little more make-up, and then surveyed the room with some misgivings. Perhaps now that Mrs Harris was gone she could persuade Jake to spend some money on redecoration, although it was possible that he might not be able to afford such luxuries.

Coming down the stairs again, buttoning the sheepskin jacket she had worn that morning, she was surprised to find Anya waiting for her in the hall. The girl had brushed her hair and put on a clean parka over her sweater and jeans, and Joanna couldn't believe that this improvement was going to last.

'Where are you going?' she asked, checking her handbag to make sure she had everything she needed, and Anya assumed an indignant expression.

'You said you wanted to go to the village,' she replied, pushing her hands into the pockets of her parka. 'I'm here to show you the way.'

'Oh!' Joanna tried not to look as astonished as she felt. After the scene in the kitchen, the last thing she had expected was that Anya should remember what she had told her, and she wondered if their apparent truce was going to last.

'You do want to go to the village, don't you?' Anya persisted, and Joanna had to admit that she did. 'Then let's go,' suggested the girl impatiently, and with a helpless shrug Joanna agreed.

Outside, the day was quite warm, considering the time of the year, and Joanna breathed deeply, feeling quite exhilarated at her unexpected success. Still, the sharpness of the air reminded her of Anya's refuge the night before, and testing the strength of her amicability, she said:

'Weren't you cold in that hut last night? I mean, it didn't look particularly well insulated, and it was quite far up the mountain.'

'Oh, that!' Anya shrugged her thin shoulders offhandedly. 'It wasn't too bad, considering. There's an old bed in there, and a couple of old blankets. And Binzer was with me.'

As if remembering the dog's companionship, she put her fingers to her mouth and emitted a piercing whistle as they reached the gates, and both dogs came bounding towards them, their shaggy hair falling untidily into their eyes.

'How on earth can you tell them apart?' exclaimed Joanna, half protestingly, as the dogs almost overbalanced her in their enthusiasm, and Anya turned a scornful face in her direction.

'Binnie is a bitch,' she declared, making the most obvious distinction. 'They are different, you know, dogs and bitches. Just like human beings.'

Joanna endeavoured not to get annoyed. 'So they are,' she countered lightly. 'I'm sorry, I didn't notice.'

Anya looked as though she would have liked to say more, but she didn't, turning out of the gate with the dogs at her heels, following the track down towards the stream.

'I—where are you going?' asked Joanna rather doubtfully, and then felt all her apprehensions return as Anya answered.

'You wanted to be shown the short cut to the village, didn't you?' she remarked innocently. 'Well, this is the way. Come on, I'll direct you.'

Joanna hesitated, hanging back, irritated at the feeling of disappointment she was experiencing. Obviously Anya had every intention of showing her the path by the stream, and while it was possible that she didn't know it was partially flooded, it was also highly unlikely. For a moment Joanna was tempted to tell her that Matt had already explained the situation to her, but then a desire to thwart the girl overcame all else. She would let Anya show her to the stream. She would let her think she was as ignorant of the dangers as Anya apparently thought her. And when she had gone, as she obviously would, she would double back and take the path through the copse.

The stream was considerably broader than its normal width, tumbling recklessly on its way, noisy as it negotiated the stones that impeded its progress. In summer, Joanna guessed its banks would be a mass of brilliant colour, but right now the slopes were muddy and even the grass looked sad, clinging to the earth in grim survival.

'That's the way,' Anya indicated, pointing to the footpath that soon wound out of sight along the bank. 'It's a bit muddy, but it will bring you out at Piper's Bridge, which is just outside the village.'

'All right,' Joanna nodded. 'Thank you.' She paused. 'You—er—you're not coming with me?'

'I don't think so, thanks.' Anya shifted restlessly from one foot to the other. 'Daddy wouldn't like it if the dogs ran wild in the village. I'd better take them back.'

Joanna shrugged. 'As you like. See you later, then.'

'Yes, later,' agreed Anya, hiding a smirk, and Joanna forced a grateful smile before starting on her way.

She wondered how far Anya expected her to get before she lost her balance and slipped into the stream. The water would be freezing, and she could imagine the girl's delight if she had to come squelching back to the house, soaked to the skin. She wondered what excuse she would give her father, and decided that so far as Anya was concerned the end justified any punishment she might have to take.

Joanna waited until she was sure that Anya must have reached Ravengarth, and then turned back. But as she did so she saw the boundary of the copse almost directly above her, and realised that she could reach the trees by climbing the slope, and thus avoid approaching the house again.

It was a damp climb, negotiating as it did knee-high grasses that soaked the legs of her pants and left them wet and uncomfortable. Even so, it was worth it to picture Anya's face on her return with the groceries, particularly as she had no intention of telling her she had taken another route.

She skirted the trees, calculating that Matt's directions would bring her to the field directly to her left. Sure enough, there was a stile, just as he had described, and she jumped down into the bristling stubble beyond with a feeling of achievement.

Then she frowned. Matt's instructions had been intended to bring her out into the lane beyond the farm buildings, but the track alongside the hedge she was presently following would bring her to the back of the buildings themselves, and even as she stopped, biting her lip, not sure which direction she ought to take, a Land Rover seemed to appear from nowhere, and came bumping over the field towards her.

She stood still, realising it would be undignified to do any other, and the vehicle drove up to her to stop with a squeal of brakes. A young man climbed down from the driving seat, viewing her with evident interest, and she returned his gaze coolly, refusing to look as embarrassed as she felt.

'Good afternoon.' His accent was not uncultivated, and she managed a faint smile.

'Good afternoon,' she responded. 'Am I trespassing?'

He grinned. 'As a matter of fact, you are, but don't let it worry you. I detect you're not from these parts.' His eyes dropped down her to rest on the damp legs of her trousers. 'What have you been doing? Wading in the beck?'

Joanna sighed, glancing back over her shoulder. 'Avoiding doing so,' she replied ruefully. 'I climbed up from the stream, if that's what you mean. The grass is very long and wet.'

'I see.' He clearly didn't, but he had accepted her explanation. 'So where were you headed? Heronsfoot?'

'Heronsfoot?' Joanna grimaced. 'Oh, no—Ravensmere.'

'Ravensmere?' He looked surprised. 'I see.'

Joanna frowned. 'I'm not going in the wrong direction, am I? I thought the village was down there.' She pointed beyond the farm buildings to where a narrow lane could be seen, winding down towards a collection of rooftops and the unmistakable sheen of water.

'It is.' The man looked slightly discomfited. 'I was just surprised, that's all. I'm afraid I didn't realise you'd walked all the way from Heronsfoot.'

Joanna looked puzzled now. 'I haven't,' she protested. 'I'm not a hiker, if that's what you think.'

'Well, I didn't think that at first, I will admit,' he conceded, half apologetically. 'But the only habitation other than ours in these parts is Ravengarth, and I know you can't be from there.'

'Oh, but I am.' Joanna ignored his astonished expression, and hurried on. 'I'm employed by Mr Sheldon. I'm An— Antonia's new governess.'

'Good lord!' The young man was obviously taken aback, and Joanna wondered how well he knew the Sheldons. 'Well, you're certainly not my idea of what a governess should look like, so perhaps I may be forgiven for making the error.'

Joanna accepted the implied compliment without comment, and realising she was wasting a lot of time when she had the journey to the village and back still to accomplish, she said: 'Perhaps you could direct me the way to the village, if you don't mind. I'm afraid I appear to have mistaken the directions I was given.'

'What? Oh, sure.' He seemed fascinated by the combination of slanted green eyes and gold-streaked brown hair, loosening again from its knot after the exertions of her climb. 'But we should introduce ourselves, don't you think? I mean, as we're going to be neighbours, so to speak. I'm Paul Trevor, and this is my father's farm.'

Joanna hesitated, and then said abruptly: 'How do you do, Mr Trevor. I'm Joanna Seton. But if you don't mind, we won't waste time in pleasantries right now. These pants are soaking, and I'd really like to get back and change.'

'Hell, yes!' His eyes dropped to the offending cords, clinging to her slender legs. 'But look——' he glanced up at her again, 'why don't you come home with me and let my mother dry them out for you? I know she'd like to meet you. We don't get many visitors around these parts, not at this time of the year anyway. Then afterwards I could run you down to the village in the Land Rover to get whatever it is you need.'

'Oh, really, I couldn't put you to that trouble,' Joanna began, but he assured her it was no trouble at all.

'Someone should have told you the path along by the beck was flooded,' he exclaimed, obviously imagining she had been trying to reach the village that way, and at his words, the recollection of Anya's intentions came surging back into her mind. It would do her good to wonder why Joanna hadn't come hurrying back to the house, and if Paul Trevor chose to drive her back to Ravengarth, so much the better.

'All right,' she said now, ruefully brushing the damp blades of grass from her knees. 'If you're sure your parents won't mind.'

'They'll be delighted, believe me,' he exclaimed, offering her a seat in the Land Rover, and with a smile she climbed in beside him.

The farmhouse was one of the buildings she had seen when she climbed over the stile. Set at right angles to a barn with a cowbyre beyond, and general outhouses fronting them across a paved courtyard, it formed the central bar of a three-sided rectangle, which would provide coolness in summer, and protection in winter. There were dogs here, too, that scattered the hens as Paul drove into the yard, and somewhere the lowing of cows indicated that afternoon milking was almost due.

This was the back of the house, Joanna realised, and they crossed the yard to a large kitchen that smelled deliciously of home baking. Although it was not much more modern in design than the kitchen at Ravengarth, everything shone with the evidence of much polishing, and she thought how much more pleasant it would be to work in surroundings like these.

Paul's mother must have heard the Land Rover, for she came into the kitchen from the hall beyond, just as Paul and Joanna entered from outside. At least, Joanna assumed she was his mother, sharing as she did her son's fair good looks, his solid youth replaced by spreading middle age. Her hair was only slightly grey, and her round face was virtually unlined, revealing that she probably enjoyed her own cooking as much as anyone. She wore a navy blue dress and a flowered apron, and her expression held mild interest as she surveyed the young woman with her son.

'We've got a visitor, Ma,' Paul told her easily, confirming Joanna's identification. 'She's from Ravengarth, and her name's Joanna Seton. Joanna?' He waited for her silent approval. 'This is my mother.'

'How do you do, Mrs Trevor.'

Joanna restrained herself from offering her hand when the older woman made no attempt to do so. If she hadn't known that it couldn't possibly be so, she would have said there was disapproval in Mrs Trevor's attitude, and she began to wish she had not allowed Paul to persuade her to come here.

'From Ravengarth, you say,' his mother remarked now, looking at her son with some irritation. 'You'd be some relative of the Sheldons, then?'

'No,' It was Paul who answered her, his blue eyes wide and impatient. 'She's the new governess, believe it or not. For Sheldon's daughter. But as you can see, she got wet climbing up from the stream, and I suggested she come here to dry off. Surely there's a pair of Barbara's slacks around somewhere that she could borrow while we dry her own.'

'Oh, I see.' The air of disapproval, if that was what it was, disappeared like magic. 'I'm sorry, Miss Seton, I didn't notice you were wet. Of course you must get changed, and while your trousers are drying, we'll have a cup of tea.'

Joanna hesitated. 'I was on my way to the village,' she began, realising this was going to take longer than she had thought, but Mrs Trevor was not perturbed.

'Paul will run you down to the village,' she declared, and her son exchanged an I-told-you-so look with Joanna. 'There's plenty of time. Now, come along upstairs with me, and I'll sort you out something to wear.'

It was kind of them to bother, but as the afternoon wore on, Joanna began to get uneasy. What time had Matt said Jake would be back? Four o'clock? Five? She couldn't remember, and she hoped he would not disapprove of her taking tea with the Trevors.

Mrs Trevor liked to gossip, but that much was obvious, but Joanna succeeded in turning most of her questions without giving too much away. Strangely, she was reluctant to tell them of the lack of success she was having with Anya, and their evident interest in Jake's affairs was tinged with an unusual amount of hostility. It was this Joanna had sensed on her arrival, she realised, and she guessed his isolation, his detachment from the community, had aroused resentment as well as curiosity.

In the event, Paul went down to the village alone, carrying with him the list of things she needed. The trousers Mrs Trevor had loaned her proved to be much too big for her slim hips, and as her own pants were not yet dry, he suggested the alternative. Joanna had no choice but to agree, though the feeling was growing stronger every minute that she should not be here.

It was about a quarter to five when Joanna heard the sound of the Land Rover returning, and rose to her feet in some relief, eager to be on her way. But when a man in his early fifties, and wearing a warehouse coat and rubber boots, came into the living room where they had been taking afternoon tea, her disappointment was almost palpable. This, of course, was Paul's father, she realised, having heard from Mrs Trevor about her husband, and her married daughter, whose trousers Joanna had borrowed, and a younger son, Andrew, who was presently away at agricultural college, and she endeavoured not to look as crestfallen as she felt. But Mr Trevor was not alone. Another man was following, and her heart flipped a nervous beat as she recognised the hard, unyielding features of her employer. In the shadows of the hall his scarred face possessed a brooding malevolence, and she gazed at him helplessly as Paul's father made the explanations.

CHAPTER FIVE

'I met Mr Sheldon in the lane,' Mr Trevor said, exchanging a meaningful glance with his wife. 'He—er—he said he was looking for this young lady, I think.' He favoured Joanna with a smile. 'Leastways, when I told him young Paul had brought a young woman up to the house, he seemed to think she might be the same.'

'Hello, Mr Sheldon.' Joanna decided to remove any doubt as her employer halted in the doorway. 'I didn't realise you'd be back yet. I'm sorry if you were beginning to wonder where I was.'

Jake's mouth was set in a straight, uncompromising line. 'Do you have a coat?' he demanded harshly, showing little regard for the demands of courtesy, and Joanna had barely started to explain when Mrs Trevor interrupted her.

'Joanna got her trousers wet climbing up from the beck, Mr Sheldon,' she exclaimed, getting to her feet. She had adopted the familiarity during the course of the afternoon, and Joanna had had no objection until now when Jake's lips thinned accordingly. 'I'm sure you can see, the slacks she's wearing at the moment belonged to my daughter Barbara, and they're miles too big for her.' She allowed herself a small, slightly nervous chuckle. 'It's our fault she's been delayed. I insisted she stay for tea, and Paul's down at the village this moment, getting the things you needed.'

Joanna's face was a blaze of colour, but Jake showed no sign of remorse at her discomfiture. 'I'm sorry you've been troubled, Mrs Trevor,' he observed flatly. 'I had no idea—Miss Seton had any intention of going to the village, or I would have saved her the trouble.' Brooding yellow eyes turned in Joanna's direction. 'Now, if you're ready ...'

His meaning was obvious, but Joanna couldn't understand why he should be so angry with her. What had she done after all? Just taken tea with a neighbour! Nothing so very dreadful about that, surely! He had no right to come here and act as if she was some kind of kept creature who had managed to escape from custody.

'I can't go yet,' she declared tersely, trying to keep her temper in spite of her indignation, and his brows arched.

'No?'

'No,' she retorted, glancing apologetically at Mrs Trevor. 'Er—Paul's not back yet.'

Jake's lips compressed. 'Then perhaps you could change your trousers, and I'll take you to meet him,' he suggested, his eyes as bleak as his tone, and with another silent plea for understanding to the Trevors, she hurried out of the room. She had to pass him to do so, and her heart pounded a trifle erratically as she met that hard unflinching gaze. It didn't help to know that despite the discrepancy in their ages— Paul was at least ten or twelve years younger than Jake— the older man possessed a strength and virility the younger man did not, and Paul's good looks faded into insignificance when compared to Jake's hard features.

She heard Mrs Trevor endeavouring to make conversation with their unexpected guest as she hastened up the stairs, but she could not hear Jake's monosyllabic responses. She guessed he resented having to come here after her just as much as she resented the feeling of constraint his arrival had put upon her, but she couldn't excuse his treatment of her, or forgive his curtness in the face of the Trevors' cordiality.

Her trousers had dried over the radiator in the bathroom. The radiators here were slightly more modern than those at Ravengarth, but the antiquated appointments of the bathroom were not. The cistern still gurgled ominously when any water was run off it, and the clawlike feet of the bath were an obvious hazard to unguarded toes.

But Joanna scarcely noticed these things as she hurriedly changed from Barbara's stretchy slacks into her own corded pants, and gave her reflection a hasty appraisal. Her cheeks were flushed, as well they might be after sitting by the fire all afternoon, she thought, although Jake's advent had not helped, and curling tendrils of honey-brown hair had escaped from the knot to stroke her tender nape. She looked doubtful and slightly apprehensive, but she tried to school her features into some semblance of composure before going back downstairs.

Her jacket was hanging on the banister at the foot of the stairs, and she hastily slipped this on before making her presence known again. Jake was still standing in the doorway to the living room, resisting all offers the Trevors were making to take tea, or something stronger, or even to sit down. When Joanna appeared he turned in evident relief, and with a brief nod of farewell urged her impatiently towards the kitchen and ultimately the yard beyond.

Joanna tried to offer her thanks, and was relieved to see that Mr and Mrs Trevor did not appear to be offended by her employer's brusque behaviour.

'Come and see us again,' exclaimed Mrs Trevor warmly, 'and bring the little girl with you. Now that we've all got to know one another, perhaps we can be good neighbours.'

'Perhaps she'd like to ride one of the horses,' suggested Mr Trevor thoughtfully. 'They're not thoroughbreds, you understand,' this to Jake, 'but they'd give her a comfortable ride.'

'It's very kind of you, Mr Trevor, but——'

'We may just do that,' Joanna interrupted him, before he could refuse their offer, casting him a look af angry resentment. 'I doubt if Anya's ever had a chance of riding. Thank you very much.'

The Range Rover was standing in the yard, and Joanna guessed that this was what she had heard earlier, when she had imagined it was Paul. However, before Jake could impel her across the pavings and into the vehicle, the Land Rover did indeed pull into the yard behind it, and Paul climbed out carrying a cardboard box containing the groceries she had ordered. He looked astonished to see Jake standing impatiently beside Joanna, but he managed to hide his reaction, and came confidently towards them.

'I got everything you asked for, Joanna,' he said, giving her the benefit of his warm smile. Then he looked at Jake. 'Hello, Sheldon. How are you? We don't often see you around here.'

Jake thrust out his hands and took the box from the younger man. 'Thank you, Trevor, I'm very grateful to you.' But he didn't look it when his hard gaze quizzed Joanna. 'Did you pay for these things? Or have you opened an account?'

'I paid for them,' declared Joanna resentfully, giving Paul a rueful smile. 'We'll sort it out later,' she added, making an expressive gesture which she hoped he would understand. 'When we have more time.'

'How much did you spend?' Jake persisted, turning back to the younger man, but Paul merely shook his head.

'I'll give Joanna the change later,' he remarked, obviously enjoying the other man's frustration, and without another word, Jake strode towards the Range Rover.

'See you soon,' Paul murmured, taking one of Joanna's hands between both of his, and grinning conspiratorially down at her. 'Don't let him bully you. You're not his possession. I'll get in touch in a day or two.'

'All right.' Joanna smiled again, and with another word of thanks to Paul's mother and father, she hastened after her employer.

Jake's face was grim as he reversed out of the yard, and then accelerated down the track to the lane Joanna had seen from the field earlier. It was obvious they would have to drive round by the village to reach the road that led up to Ravengarth, and she prepared herself to answer the censure she was sure was to come.

Jake didn't speak, however. He seemed totally absorbed with driving the vehicle, and in the end Joanne herself had to break the uneasy silence between them.

'Was there any need for you to be so rude to the Trevors?' she demanded, unable to prevent the indignation she felt from spilling over from her tongue. 'I may be your employee, but I'm not your slave, and there was no need for you to treat them as if they were to blame for my absence! Perhaps you'd have been better pleased if I'd come back to the house as Anya intended, soaked to the skin and shivering with——'

'If you had had the decency to inform me that you intended to spend the afternoon gossiping with the Trevors, then perhaps you would have some excuse for that statement!' he snapped angrily, overriding her passionate tirade. 'Are you aware that for fully an hour after my return, I was convinced you must have been swept downstream into the lake, and I was on the point of calling out the rescue services when I met Trevor coming down from the farm!'

Joanna gulped, and stared at him disbelievingly. 'Swept downstream into the lake!' she echoed. 'Don't be ridiculous!'

The Range Rover lurched to a shuddering halt as Jake stood on his brakes, and she trembled a little fearfully as he turned fully to look at her. 'Don't you ever say that to me again!' he grated angrily, long brown fingers punishing the steering wheel, as he would probably have liked to punish her throat. 'How dare you sit there and reproach me for my conduct at the farm, when only minutes before I'd suspected you were dead! How do you think I felt, walking in there and finding you sitting drinking tea, as if we weren't out of our minds with worry about you!'

Joanna swallowed rather convulsively. 'That—that's silly,' she exclaimed. 'I—Matt knew I was going to the village. So did Anya.' Her lips tightened in remembrance.

'But you didn't get to the village, did you?' demanded Jake savagely. 'And Matt told you to use the field path, not the path by the stream, that's already subsided into the water in places.'

Joanna held up her head. 'I didn't use the path by the stream,' she declared, and his mouth hardened.

'Then how did your trousers get wet?'

Joanna sighed. 'Does it matter? They did. And that's all there is to it.'

Jake's fingers released the wheel to slide wearily through his dark hair. 'I know about Anya directing you to the stream,' he declared. 'You needn't imagine you're protecting her by remaining silent on that score.' He looked at her broodingly, one hand resting at the nape of his neck. 'In God's name, why did you do it?'

'Why did I do what?' Joanna found she was more disturbed by the probing appeal in his lean face than by the angry aggression he had exhibited previously, and he moved his broad shoulders in a helpless gesture.

'You knew we would worry about you,' he stated slowly. 'You must have known that when you didn't come back, Anya would get frightened.'

'Frightened?' That contingency had not occurred to her. 'But why frightened? The stream's not like a river. It's not deep enough to drown anyone!'

'No?' Jake's tawny eyes bored into hers. 'Then let me offer you an alternative. Suppose you'd taken the path by the stream. Suppose Matt hadn't warned you about its being flooded, and you'd gone on?' He paused to allow his words to sink in. 'Suppose a section of the path had crumbled beneath you, and you'd been thrown into the water? What kind of chance do you think you would have had, if you'd hit your head on a stone and been knocked unconscious? The force of that stream in flood is capable of carrying a body down into the lake. I know. Sheep have been drowned that way.'

Joanna pressed her unsteady lips together. 'I didn't know that.'

'You didn't think, did you?'

Joanna sighed. 'How was I to know what you'd think?' She shook her head. 'All right, so I may have thought of teaching Anya a lesson, but I never intended to frighten her—or anyone.'

Jake studied her anxious face for another long moment, then he turned slowly back to the wheel. 'So you understand now why I was in no mood to exchange pleasantries with my neighbours.' He thrust the car heavily into gear once more. 'I had more—pressing things on my mind.'

Joanna looked at him unhappily. 'And you've been searching for me for an hour?'

'Something like that,' he agreed offhandedly. 'I found your footsteps in the mud by the stream, but then they disappeared. It didn't occur to me that you might have climbed up to the Trevors' place. It's a steep ascent, and the grass is almost waist-high. You must have got soaked!'

'I did,' Joanna agreed with a sigh, and he gave her another assessing glance.

'That's how you got wet.' It was a statement, not a question, but she nodded. 'How foolish of me not to think of that.' He shook his head. 'I seem to have jumped to all the wrong conclusions.' His lips twisted. 'Still, I've no doubt you enjoyed yourself. The Trevors have no love for me. I don't invite confidences and I don't give them, and they, like the rest of the village, imagine I'm mentally as well as physically scarred.'

'Don't say that!' Joanna's response was angry, a reason to expunge some of the helpless frustration she was now feeling. 'They're curious about you, of course, but that's just their way. They didn't mean any harm. And if you think I've spent the afternoon discussing you, you're very much mistaken.'

'Ah, no, I didn't say that,' he contradicted sardonically. 'I'm sure you and—Paul, is it?—had more interesting things to talk about. However, I'd deem it a favour if you didn't encourage Anya to go there. Kind though they may be, I have no desire for her to get involved with any of the people around here, but of course, I can't dictate what you do in your own time.'

'Thank you.' Joanna pursed her lips. It was scarcely a concession, and she wished she dared ask why he was restricting the child in this way. Maybe if Anya met more people, had more interests, she would be less of a problem, but obviously right now was not the time to make her feelings felt.

The journey back to Ravengarth was soon over. They bumped down the track to the copse, and Jake opened and closed the gate before driving the last few hundred yards to the house. He turned into the cobbled yard, switched off the engine, and then thrust open his door without saying another word.

Joanna shook her head as she gathered her belongings preparatory to getting out also. Was it really only yesterday she had come here? she asked herself incredulously. Some-

how it seemed so much longer than that since she had met
Jake Sheldon.

It was in bed later that she found the time to review her
situation once again. She had had little opportunity since
Jake brought her back from the Trevors to permit herself
such a luxury, but at last, in her room, she was able to
assimilate and digest the events of the day.

Her only contact with Anya since her return was a muttered apology, delivered in her pyjamas, in the presence of
her father. Jake had brought his daughter down from her
room, where apparently she had been sent on pain of a
beating should she disobey him again, and she had stood
before Joanna and mumbled the words, with tears of morti-
fication and resentment glimmering in her blue eyes. She
knew Joanna had won another battle, and her defences were
crumbling in the face of this concerted onslaught.

Of Jake himself Joanna had seen almost as little. Her
return had been greeted with obvious relief by Matt Coulston, and she had given the old man a special smile of
apology, that he should have been worried, too.

'I didn't realise you'd be so anxious,' Joanna told him,
feeling contrite. 'I'm sorry if I've wasted your time.'

'Oh, I did some digging like you said,' Matt assured her
airily, and it was left to Jake to look puzzled at this unexpected announcement. 'The young lady suggested I should
start digging the vegetable plot over,' Matt went on to
explain, much to Joanna's chagrin. 'Just to keep me busy,
so to speak. While you were away.'

Jake's mouth had compressed at this, but he had made
no comment, and Joanna had gone indoors, realising with
a pang that there was no one but herself to prepare the
evening meal.

In the event, Jake did not eat at home. He took Anya back
upstairs after making her apologise, and then came down
again as Joanna was unpacking the groceries Paul had col-
lected for her. He came into the kitchen as she was putting
some cheese into the refrigerator, and noticing the pans al-

ready set on the cooker, asked what she thought she was doing.

'Making supper,' she answered smoothly, refusing to be ruffled by his dark, aggressive countenance. 'I was going to cook the chicken Matt plucked for me, but it's a bit late now to prepare a proper meal, so we'll have to make do with tinned soup and gammon.'

'I did not employ you to cook my meals,' Jake averred, his expression twisted with irritation, and Joanna looked at him squarely.

'Then who is going to do it?' she asked, tilting her head, and his eyes narrowed at the implied criticism.

'I'll go into the village,' he said shortly. 'There's a fish shop there. We can have fish and chips this evening, and tomorrow I'll try the employment exchange in Penrith.'

Joanna sighed. 'I for one don't want fish and chips,' she declared, her nose wrinkling at the thought of all that grease. 'And I don't think Anya should have such a thing before bed. I can easily heat the soup, and if I grill the gammon, there are tins of pineapple——'

'Thank you, but I do not require you to practice your culinary abilities on me,' Jake retorted coldly. 'And while we're discussing food, I should point out that we do not shop at the village store. Whatever you thought we needed could have waited until I go into Penrith tomorrow, and in future——'

'There was no bread,' Joanna had interrupted him, then, her eyes sparkling. 'No bread, no butter and no flour. Your housekeeper was as good at keeping a full larder as she was at everything else! And I do not intend to starve just to please you!'

Jake's eyes were glacial now, and she realised she was once again going too far.

'And you did pay for this food, didn't you?' he demanded, glancing around. 'I prefer not to appear a pauper in fact as well as appearance. How much do I owe you?'

'I paid,' said Joanna, a little shortly. 'But you don't have to worry——'

'Thank you, but I prefer to pay my debts,' he retorted

coldly. 'In spite of your obvious opinion of my financial situation, I am reasonably solvent, and if this place denies that assumption, put it down to a disappointing lack of interest on my behalf.'

Joanna licked her dry lips. 'It's nothing to do with me, Mr Sheldon——'

'But you've made it so,' he countered bleakly, pulling his wallet out of his pocket. 'Here,' he tossed several five-pound notes on to the table. 'That should cover it, and anything else you need in the immediate future. And now— if you'll excuse me,' and he left before she could either thank him or deplore his extravagance.

He appeared once more as she was carrying a tray containing Anya's supper out of the kitchen, on her way to the child's room. With a curt: 'I'll take that,' he lifted it out of her hands, and she returned to the kitchen and her own lonely meal with a feeling of intense frustration.

Now, lying in the darkness, she couldn't help wondering where Jake was and what he was doing. She had heard the Land Rover depart as she was taking half-hearted mouthfuls of celery soup, but although she had waited, as she had done the night before, he had not returned. She hoped he had got himself something to eat. She doubted he had had anything all day, and the realisation that she was beginning to feel a sense of responsibility towards him made her bury her head in the pillow and silence her thoughts.

There was no one to wake her the following morning, but surprisingly, Joanna was awake at seven a.m. Despite the fact that it was a dull morning outside and the light was still grey and uninspiring, she felt no remorse at getting out of bed, and after a hasty sluice in the bath with delightfully hot water, she dressed in jeans and a sweater and went downstairs. She really would have to find time to unpack today, she thought ruefully, her overflowing suitcase catching her eyes as she brushed her silky hair before the dressing table mirror. And to write to her mother, too, she determined, feeling a pang of compunction at the realisation that she had hardly thought of her own family since coming to Ravengarth.

Deciding she did not have time to secure her hair in the knot, which had proved unsatisfactory the day before anyway, she merely tied it back with a black ribbon and restricted the use of cosmetics to a colourless lip lustre. Somehow it seemed pointless spending ages on eye make-up when she intended to spend the morning cleaning up the kitchen. She was totally unaware that the curling bronze lashes had a beauty all their own, without the darkening accent of mascara, and her skin was smooth and pearly soft, and required little but a moisturiser to keep it so.

It was certainly chilly as she ran down the stairs, but she found to her relief that the kitchen was deliciously warm. Evidently Jake had fed the stove the night before, and it was glowing brightly, the obvious reason for the hot water she had enjoyed earlier.

Despite his objections to her buying food in the village, someone had cut bread from the fresh loaf and spread it with butter from the pack she had purchased. She guessed from the plate and cup left to dry on the draining board that Jake had already had toast and coffee, and the faint aroma of burnt bread seemed to confirm this. She plugged in the electric kettle to make herself some coffee and pondered the possibility that Jake might eat a more substantial meal later, and then decided she had no authority to act on this presumption, and concentrated instead on getting the place clean and tidy.

Unused as she was to housework, it wasn't easy deciding which chore she ought to tackle first, but eventually she set about the most obvious tasks of cleaning the sink and working surfaces, and washing the floor which had about a month's accumulation of dirt on it. She ate her breakfast as she worked, stopping every now and then to take a mouthful of toast and a swallow of coffee before getting on, and by the time Anya dragged her feet into the room she had made a distinct improvement in its appearance.

'Where's Daddy?' Clearly Anya saw nothing of note in her efforts, and rinsing her hands at the sink, Joanna endeavoured not to feel aggrieved.

'I'm not sure where he is,' she replied, adopting a bright

air of competence, 'but if you want breakfast, then you'd better tell me what you'd like.'

Anya frowned. 'Isn't Mrs Harris coming back?' she asked, and this time Joanna guessed she was not being obscurely critical.

'No,' she replied, refilling the kettle and plugging it in again. 'Your father's going to employ another housekeeper, but until he does, I shall do what I can.'

Anya sniffed, a habit Joanna was sure now she had picked up from Mrs Harris, and rubbed her nose on the sleeve of her sweater. It was rather a nice sweater, or it would be if it was clean, and it reminded Joanna of the pile of dirty washing still waiting to be done.

'Did you make my supper last night?' Anya asked now, her expression brooding, and when Joanna nodded: 'Don't you know how to do anything else but open tins?' she exclaimed scornfully. 'I could make the meals you make. Anyone could!'

Once again Joanna kept her temper with difficulty. 'As you probably are aware, I intended to make a proper meal for all of us last night,' she said pleasantly, 'only a certain person who shall be nameless gave me faulty directions to the village in the hope that I'd fall into the stream!'

Anya's thin face flushed. 'I didn't hope that at all,' she denied hotly. 'There is a path to the village alongside the stream——'

'—which you knew was flooded!' Joanna declared steadily. 'Look, I don't intend to get involved in arguments over the whys and wherefores of what might have happened. Fortunately, Matt had warned me of the dangers——'

'You let me think you didn't know the way,' Anya protested indignantly. 'You tricked me!'

'And isn't that exactly what you were trying to do to me?'

Anya bent her head. 'I came back. I looked for you. But you'd disappeared.'

'Well, I'm sorry.' Joanna had not known this. 'But if you will persist in lighting fireworks, you have to be prepared for them to backfire.'

Anya hesitated. 'You went to Trevors', didn't you?

Daddy told me. He said you'd been there all the time. Why did you go there? Do you know them? Did you intend to go there all along?'

'Heavens, no.' Patiently, Joanna explained how she had climbed up through the wet grass and met Paul Trevor, and why he had suggested she come home with him. She glossed over Jake's arrival, and their subsequent journey back to Ravengarth, and merely let the child know the facts of what happened.

Anya hunched her shoulders, shoving her hands into the pockets of her jeans. 'Daddy was furious,' she declared, though not with any pleasure at the recollection. 'He said you might have drowned. You wouldn't have drowned, would you, Miss Seton?' She paused as if to give more emphasis to her last statement. 'Witches always float—I read it in a book.'

Joanna shook her head, regarding Anya with mild exasperation. 'Now don't pretend you think I'm a witch,' she stated firmly. 'You're far too intelligent to believe a thing like that, and if I were, do you think I'd be here, washing floors and cooking meals? I'd just wave my magic wand and get some genie to do it for me, wouldn't I? So let's stop this silliness and get down to plain speaking. Do you want any breakfast or don't you? And where does your father keep your textbooks?'

Anya tipped her head on one side. 'Do you really think I'm intelligent?' she exclaimed, and Joanna realised that of all the things she had said, that had had the most impact.

'Of course I do,' she said now, setting a clean plate and cup and saucer on the table. 'Now, would you like some ham and eggs, or poached egg on toast, or just toast and marmalade?'

Anya was still regarding her doubtfully. 'The others—the other governesses I had, they all said I was backward,' she declared slowly. 'One of them even said I was men—mentally retracted.'

'Retarded,' Joanna corrected flatly, and she shook her head. 'Well, you're not, take my word for it. But if your school work is poor, that can only be remedied by your own efforts, no one else's.'

Anya pulled a face. 'I don't like school. At least, not the schools here. And they didn't like me.'

Joanna shrugged. 'If you make a nuisance of yourself ...'

'I didn't. Not all the time, anyway. They just make me so mad!'

Joanna knew she was treading on tentative ground now. 'Did they?' she asked quietly. 'Why?'

But Anya wasn't listening to her. 'It was different before, in London. I liked school then. Daddy used to drive me to school every morning, on his way to work——'

She broke off suddenly as if remembering to whom she was speaking, and Joanna, eager not to destroy that tenuous beginning, quickly asked her what she would like to eat again, thus preventing any backlash.

She decided to have poached egg on toast, and was swallowing the last morsels when her father came in at the back door. The morning had turned to rain, and the steady drizzle had left droplets of water gleaming on his dark hair, dampening the shoulders of the brown tweed hacking jacket he was wearing. Joanna, used now to those dark scarred features, found his appearance disturbing, and she turned back to the dishes she had been washing in the sink, hoping he did not suspect the emotion he aroused in her. It was crazy, she thought irritably, scouring a saucepan more vigorously than it demanded. He was a man almost twenty years her senior, with a grown-up son to boot, she reminded herself severely, recognising the symptoms of physical attraction and resenting them. She was allowing the unavoidable intimacies of the situation to influence her reaction to him, and the sooner he employed another housekeeper, the better. Then she could take her proper place in the household, and direct all her attentions to the task for which she had come here.

Now, Jake's eyes narrowed as they took in the domestic scene before him, and his first words helped Joanna to dispel the sense of awareness she was experiencing.

'I thought I asked you not to interfere in matters which don't concern you, Miss Seton,' he declared, closing the outer door and advancing into the room. He cast his daughter a reproving look and then added: 'Anya is quite capable of preparing her own breakfast, and while I appreciate your looking after yourself for the moment, I would prefer it if you didn't behave as if I'd hired you as a home help.'

Joanna turned, wiping her soapy hands on a towel and then resting back against the sink behind her. 'Why shouldn't I help, Mr Sheldon,' she asked, refusing to give him the pleasure of provoking her. 'I'm not entirely useless, as you can see, and if I'm not complaining, why should you?'

'I don't want you writing home to your mother, telling her that I've turned you into some kind of drudge,' he snapped. 'My sister already imagines we live like peasants: imagine her satisfaction if your mother confirms that supposition!'

Joanna gasped. 'You don't suppose I'd complain about doing something I chose to do, do you?' she exclaimed. 'And in any case, if I were to explain the situation here, my mother would probably insist I return home right away!'

His mouth twisted. 'That's the truth!'

Joanna sighed. 'Is it? I don't think you quite understand——'

'Oh, I understand very well. If you described the state of this place to your mother, I've no doubt she would be horrified——'

'I'm not talking about the state of this place!' Joanna interrupted him, unable to keep the note of exasperation out of her voice. 'But you are a widower, Mr Sheldon, and therefore unmarried, and it might seem—improper to my mother that we should be sharing the same house.'

The blood running up under his skin darkened the already swarthy cast of his features as he stared at her. It was the first time she had seen a man colour like that, and it disturbed her almost as much as his words did.

'You're young enough to be my daughter, Miss Seton,' he got out at last, harshly, pushing impatient fingers through his hair. 'And despite my obvious shortcomings,

I'm not a complete Philistine! Your—virtue, if that isn't too old-fashioned a word, is safe with me!'

Joanna's face burned now, and she was glad when Anya, who had watched this interchange with evident interest, asked: 'What's a Philistine, Daddy?'

'It's not important,' he muttered, glancing broodingly about the kitchen, as if just noticing how much cleaner it looked. 'I've got to go into Penrith this morning, and before I go, I want your assurance that you'll not give Miss Seton any more trouble.'

Anya swallowed the remains of the orange juice Joanna had given her to finish, and wiped her mouth with her hand. 'Can't I come with you?' she demanded in a plaintive voice, but he shook his head.

'I've got to try and find another housekeeper,' he explained, his tone softening slightly. 'I should be back by tea time. But if I'm not, try and behave yourself. I don't want to have to punish you a third time, do you understand?'

'Yes, Daddy.' Anya hunched her shoulders defensively, and Joanna hoped she intended to keep her promise.

'Would you like some coffee before you go?' she asked Jake now, hoping to delay the moment when she and Anya would have to come to terms with one another, but he shook his head.

'I'd better get started,' he replied, his eyes avoiding hers after that unsettling personal exchange. 'However, I want to see Matt before I go, so if there's anything you'd like me to get for you, please make a list.' He paused. 'You might start the lessons today, if you have the time.' His tone was sardonic. 'That was something I intended to discuss with you last night.'

'There is something I have to ask you,' Joanna ventured, casting a doubtful look in Anya's direction, and he faced her reluctantly, the tawny eyes veiled by the long lashes that were the only incongruous aspect of that harsh visage. 'Where do you keep Anya's school books? The textbooks she uses? Only I'd like to find out how advanced she is in English and arithmetic before we begin any formal lessons.'

'They're in my desk, in the library,' he replied, turning away as soon as he decently could. 'You can find them for yourself. There's nothing private in there. You can even use the library to work in, if you like. That's up to you.'

'Thank you,' Joanna nodded, and with evident relief, he turned towards the door once more. 'Oh——' She remembered one last thing, and he turned half impatiently. 'Yes?'

'It's milk,' Joanna explained. 'I mean, you obviously don't get a regular delivery——'

'We have a cow!' It was Anya's scornful young voice that answered her. 'Matt looks after her. Her name's Gertrude. He fetches the milk for us. You just tell him what you need, and the rest he uses himself or sells to Mr Page at the pub.'

'That will do, Anya.' Jake gave her a silencing look, and she relapsed into brooding melancholy. 'But it's true, we do provide our own milk and eggs, and it was my intention to buy a deep-freeze and store our own meat and vegetables, too.' He paused. 'Perhaps I will now. Mrs Harris always refused to have anything to do with frozen food.'

Joanna didn't say anything, but she guessed the late housekeeper would have maintained it was too much trouble. Mrs Harris probably found it much easier, shopping in the supermarket in Penrith, buying ready-cooked foods that required the minimum amount of preparation.

'Is that all?' Jake was opening the door as he spoke. 'As I said, write down anything you want and leave the list in here.'

Joanna nodded. 'Drive carefully,' she said, almost as an afterthought, and glimpsed the sudden hardening of his features as he closed the door behind him. It wasn't until later that she realised exactly what he must have been thinking.

CHAPTER SIX

DESPITE the miserable weather, Joanna refused to feel downhearted. She had Anya's company, at least, and while that might be a dubious blessing, she was determined not to let the little progress they had made slip away. It wasn't going to be easy, always knowing how best to approach the child, but she intended to take each minute as it came, and deal with the problems accordingly.

With Jake's departure, she ventured into the library, and was reassured when Anya followed her. But one look at the untidy apartment convinced her that they could not work in such surroundings, and with a little gesture of resignation she said:

'How are you at dusting, Anya? Could we use this morning as a lesson in housekeeping and do something to make this room more cheerful?'

Not really to her surprise, Anya was quite amenable, but what did surprise her was the girl's capacity for work when it suited her. Instead of being the hindrance Joanna had half expected, Anya toiled as hard as she did, shifting books off the shelves and dusting them vigorously, fetching and carrying, and showing none of the animosity Joanna had previously experienced.

It was impossible to make the room elegant, the shabby carpets and furnishings defied such a description, but with a fire burning in the grate, fed by the load of logs Matt provided at their request, and everywhere swept and dusted, it had a homely charm. The old man even found an armful of chrysanthemums from somewhere, and Anya arranged them in a pottery vase, and with Jake's paintings neatly stacked in one corner and the desk free of all litter, they all felt reasonably pleased with their efforts.

They had spaghetti bolognaise for lunch. Joanna had bought the spaghetti the day before, and with a savoury sauce she concocted from a tin of meat, a tin of tomatoes, some cheese and onion, and some herbs, it smelled delicious. Matt sniffed the air appreciatively when he came to fetch the milk Joanna had asked for, and on impulse she invited him to join them. They all sat around the newly-scrubbed table in the kitchen, and even Anya chatted away to the old man without any restraint at Joanna's presence.

'I remember Daddy once taking me to an Italian restaurant,' she confided, concentrating on curling the spaghetti round her fork. 'He had spaghetti whatever-it-is, but I had pizza. I wish I'd had this now.'

'It's amazing what you can do with tins,' remarked Joanna drily, unable to resist the mild taunt, and Anya actually grinned. Her pointed features had a piquant charm when she relaxed, and Joanna found herself responding.

'You going to cook that chicken I gave you for supper tonight?' Matt asked, when she got up to clear the table and she turned back to him nodding.

'I though I might make a casserole,' she said. 'It's the sort of meal than can be kept hot for a long time, just in case Mr Sheldon doesn't get back as soon as he expected.'

'Daddy said you hadn't to make our meals,' Anya put in without malice, and Joanna sighed.

'Someone has to,' she declared reasonably. 'What would you have had for lunch if I hadn't prepared it?'

Anya shrugged. 'Jam and bread, I s'pose,' she admitted, rubbing the side of her nose—a definite improvement on sniffing, Joanna felt. 'I don't mind what you do. But Daddy said——'

'Yes, I know what your father said,' Joanna retorted with a sigh, and then realised Matt was speaking again.

'Like I was saying,' he added, 'that there chicken I brought you. She's—well, she'll be a tough old bird.' He paused, looked slightly embarrassed, and then went on: 'It was different when it was Lily Harris I was dealing with. She used to overcook everything. Like as not, she'd have boiled old Gloria. But if you want a bird to roast—well, I reckon I could find you a tender young chicken, sweet as a nut, with a nice bit of flesh on its bones.'

Joanna laughed; she couldn't help it. Matt looked so hot under the collar, and it was gratifying to know that he at least had come to accept her.

'Don't worry,' she assured him gently, patting his shoulder as she passed. 'I'll cook it nice and slowly, and I know a few tricks for tenderising all kinds of meat and poultry. But thanks for the offer. I appreciate it.'

'You're not as helpless as you look, are you, Miss Joanna?' he said admiringly, levering himself up from his chair with difficulty, and she pretended to be put out.

'That's a backhanded compliment,' she protested, assuming an air of indignation, but the look they exchanged was one of understanding as he moved away from the table.

'Said you were a pretty lassie, the first time I laid eyes on you,' he declared, arching his spine with evident reluctance. 'And a stubborn one too, I'll warrant.' He grimaced. 'Got my muscles fair groaning, you have, with all that digging yesterday. You watch out, young Anya. She's not the type to give up at the first obstacle, not like those other women.'

Joanna sighed, wishing he would keep those sort of comments to himself, but apart from pressing her lips a little more thinly together Anya did nothing.

'We'll see you later, Matt,' Joanna added, as he let himself out, and breathed an unconscious sigh of relief once she and Anya were alone.

The fire in the library had spread its warmth throughout the room, and the musty smell Joanna had first noticed had almost gone. In its place was the pervading perfume of the chrysanthemums, and the not unpleasant aroma of woodsmoke.

She found Anya's textbooks in the bottom drawer of Jake's desk. There were history books and geography books, an English grammar and a book of mathematical problems. The corresponding exercise books were with them, and while Anya stretched herself rather moodily in a chair beside the fire, Joanna studied her written work. Most of it was not good. There were too many errors, as well as an abundance of smudges and ink blots which gave the books an untidy appearance. What was surprising was that her spelling was excellent, as too was her attention to detail, and while other subjects merited only the briefest of essays, her English spread generously over pages and pages.

Unfortunately, someone—the last governess?—had scrawled all over the work, indicating her opinion of Anya's apparent aptitude for literacy. There were comments like 'Too long-winded' and 'Try to avoid over-dramatising' and 'What has this to do with the essay?', and as Joanna read the pages of smeared handwriting she began to see why those comments had been made. The titles of the essays bore little resemblance to what came after. Anya seemed to use the titles only as ideas to elaborate, and it was obvious that a vivid imagination supplied the rest. What previous governesses had not seemed to notice, or if they had, they had not considered it praiseworthy, was that Anya possessed a remarkable talent for storytelling, and her essays were really wonderful fairy stories, wrapped around with all the folklore she had read and learned about throughout her young life. Joanna sat back amazed at the discovery she had made, and her eyes turned to the girl staring broodingly into the fire.

'What exactly did—the other governesses say about your work, Anya?' she asked, choosing her words with caution. 'It's obvious that you didn't enjoy history or maths, but why did you say they thought you were backward?'

Anya regarded her silently for a moment, as if gauging her reactions to what she had just read, and then she shrugged. 'I'm no good at lessons any more,' she mumbled, cupping her chin on one hand, and before Joanna could ask what she meant by 'any more' she went on: 'I used to like school once, in London. The teachers there didn't think I was stupid.' She paused. 'But that was a long time ago.'

Joanna hesitated. 'But what did these governesses you've had say to you? I mean, they must have had some opinion of your work.'

Anya thought for a minute, then she said: 'Miss Towers who came first—she was the best. She used to let me write during her lessons, and I liked that. I like writing. But Daddy sacked her because I wasn't learning anything, and the other two were horrible!'

Joanna sighed. 'How were they horrible?'

Anya frowned. 'Miss Latimer used to shout. She used to get angry because I couldn't do her rotten sums, and in the end I put a rat in her bedroom and she left.'

Joanna hid her reaction to this, and said faintly: 'And the other?'

'Miss Gering?' Anya hunched her shoulders. 'She was German, not a lot older than you are, but very strict. She used to put her hair in a plait and she always wore long skirts and flat shoes. She was the worst of all. Daddy made me pay attention to her, and if I didn't, she used to tell on me.' Her mouth jutted. 'Just like you did yesterday.'

Joanna gasped. 'I didn't tell on you!' She made a help-less gesture. 'You brought what happened on yourself!'

'You told Daddy I'd taken you down to the stream,' re-torted Anya hotly.

'I did not,' Joanna objected indignantly. 'He already knew.'

Anya stared at her. 'I don't believe you.'

'That's up to you.' Joanna refused to be browbeaten. 'Nevertheless, it's true. One thing I don't do is lie.'

Anya's lashes came to veil her eyes. 'Why did you ask me about the other governesses?' she asked. 'Why do you want to know?'

Joanna took the olive branch willingly. 'I was curious, that's all. I wondered who had scribbled all over your work.'

'Oh, that was Miss Gering,' said Anya, getting up to take a look. 'She said I was too fanciful. She told Daddy I still believed in fairies.'

Joanna gave her a wry look. 'And do you?'

Anya seemed to consider her answer. 'If I said yes, would you think I was backward?'

'No.' Joanna shook her head. 'Unlike Miss Gering, I think it's necessary to keep our dreams as long as we can. So long as we don't mix up fact with fantasy. Your work——' she indicated the open book on the desk, 'your work is imaginative, but I think that's because you enjoy writing. I liked reading your stories. I'm not saying you shouldn't pay more attention to your other lessons, these other books show a pretty poor standard, but you're not backward, only under-educated.'

Anya straightened her spine and looked down at her doubtfully. 'What if I said I didn't mind being under-educated, so long as I could write my stories? Why should I have to learn geography and history? I shan't need them if I'm going to be a writer.'

Joanna shrugged. 'I should have thought, if you were going to be a writer, you'd need all sorts of information.'

'What do you mean?'

'Well, it's all right brushing aside geography and history if you're going to spend your life writing about elves and fairies. But as you get older, your writing will mature. You might like to write about other lands and other people. That's where geography comes in. Or about other times——'

'And that's history,' said Anya gloomily.

'Yes.'

The girl shook her head. 'I've never thought of that.' A faint smile touched her lips. 'And I don't think you did, until now.'

Joanna had to smile in return. 'You must admit, it is original,' she agreed, without conceit. 'So—what do you say? If I persuade your father that what you're writing is not fanciful rubbish, will you do your best to improve your other work?'

'How do you know I'll work for you, any better than for Miss Latimer or Miss Gering?'

'Because I'm more like Miss Towers,' declared Joanna firmly. 'Except that I will expect you to work, and shall expect you to make progress.'

Anya giggled. It was the first time she had relaxed so far and Joanna felt almost weak with success. 'Miss Towers was at least fifty,' she declared, 'and she wore thick horn-rimmed spectacles.'

Joanna shrugged, not at all put out. 'Well, I can find some

spectacles, if I have to,' she said, with a grimace, and with a little more enthusiasm, Anya pulled a chair to the desk.

Jake had not returned home by five o'clock and Joanna checked the casserole she had made earlier before making herself and Anya some tea. Anya had finished hers and disappeared about some business of her own when Joanna heard the sound of the Range Rover, and she unconsciously straightened her spine as Jake came into the kitchen where she was sitting. He noticed at once the tray of tea on the table in front of her, but she guessed it was the appetising aroma from the oven that caused the instinctive tightening of his lips. However, he made no immediate comment, merely closed the outer door behind him and strode rather wearily towards the glowing eye of the Aga.

Joanna watched him warm his hands for a moment, and then she got up from the table. 'Would you like some tea?' she offered, and when he turned to look at her over his shoulder: 'Don't refuse. There's plenty left, and you look as though you could do with a cup.'

Jake turned fully to face her, hands behind his back, parting the tweed hacking jacket, exposing the taut expanse of brown silk straining across his chest. It was the first time she had seen him wearing anything other than the cotton shirts and cords he wore around the farm, and she could not help admiring the way his dark brown suede pants moulded the powerful contours of his thighs. He was all muscle and bone, and Joanna's reactions to him frightened her a little. This was a contingency she had never expected, believing as her mother had done, that Jake was so much older, but although she knew that he must be nearly forty, he possessed a latent sexuality that defied age or circumstance.

There was an awful moment when she realised she had been staring, and his grim face mirrored his reactions to her fixation. It was obvious that he had got an entirely wrong impression of her numbed fascination, and in a harsh voice he said:

'What's the matter? Am I putting you off your tea? If

you just leave the things, I can pour myself a cup, and then I suggest you go and pack your belongings.'

'Pack my belongings?' Joanna's gaze was unwavering now. 'Why should I pack my belongings? I don't know what you're talking about. I'm not leaving!'

He came towards the table, long brown fingers beating an erratic tattoo on its surface. 'I think you should,' he declared steadily. 'I think it would be the best thing for all of us. Apart from Anya's obstructive behaviour, I've been unable to find anyone willing to come and work at Ravengarth, and as you pointed out, it's not suitable for an unmarried man and woman—girl—to share the same house unchaperoned.'

Joanna's eyes widened. 'You said this morning that I was young enough to be your daughter!' she reminded him. 'That it didn't matter——'

'I've had second thoughts about the matter.'

'Well, I haven't.' Joanna was feeling a little desperate now. It was all very well grumbling about the state of the house, and wishing Anya was a more normal little girl, but they were only small grievances. She didn't want to go, of that she was certain, and she feared the determination in Jake's face that saw all the wrong things in hers.

'Perhaps I was wrong to imagine anyone could make any headway with Anya,' he muttered, half to himself. 'It's been too long. And after three unsuccessful attempts, I should have realised I was wasting my time——'

'You're not! That is—I'm not.' Joanna took an involuntary step towards him, unwittingly bringing her within arm's length of his dark tormented face. Somehow she had to convince him that she was different, that she was having some success with the child. 'Mr Sheldon, I think you might reconsider when I tell you——'

'Miss Seton.' He straightened as she neared him, pushing back his shoulders and making a concerted effort to disguise his weariness. 'I'm sure you mean well, but there comes a time when even I have to admit defeat. Anya will have to go to boarding school. Somewhere there must be a school that will take her, and any hopes that I might have had for softening the blow will have to be abandoned.'

- 'Don't say that!' Joanna put out an unthinking hand and grasped his sleeve, only intent at that moment to relieve his mood of discouragement. She was hardly aware of him as a man as she stretched out her hand, only as a dispirited human being, but the minute her fingers closed on his sleeve and felt the tensing of hard muscle beneath, all detachment fled. The unconscious intimacy of her action had brought her even closer to him, closer than she had been before, and almost savagely he looked down at her, willing her to recoil from the scarred proximity of his flawed features.

But she didn't. She looked up at him half wonderingly, examining his ravaged face in detail for the first time, and realised with a sense of amazement that she couldn't imagine him any other way. She had grown accustomed to his harsh appearance, it was as much a part of him as the smooth dark virility of his hair, and those curious amber eyes, and without stopping to ponder the whys and wherefores of what she was doing, she reached up and touched his cheek with a tentative finger. It was what she had wanted to do, she realised, since their first confrontation two days ago in the library, but what she was not prepared for was his violent reaction.

'Don't do that!' he snapped, dashing her hand away, and pushing angry fingers into the collar of his shirt as if it was suddenly too tight. 'I am not a wax dummy, Miss Seton. Just because you're leaving, don't imagine that gives you the right to treat me like a museum exhibit. I don't like being touched at any time, least of all by an inquisitive adolescent with a view to relating her experiences to a morbidly avid audience!'

'I'm not leaving,' Joanna declared vehemently. 'I don't want to leave.'

'Unfortunately, one can't always do what one wants to do, Miss Seton,' he retorted, drawing a deep breath, 'As I say, Anya is my primary concern, and——'

'I know that!'

'——as it's obvious that despite the similarity in your ages, which I'd thought might be an advantage——'

'I'm twenty years old, Mr Sheldon. Not a child!'

'—you're having no success——'

'Will you listen to me!' Joanna almost shouted the words, and his surprise temporarily cut off the depressing trend of his summation. 'I *am* making some progress with Anya. I am! We've spent the whole day together, and there's been no discord. None at all!'

He studied her impatient face for a long moment without saying anything, and her temper was not improved by the awareness of the slow colour that was mounting in her cheeks. Then, as if dismissing any softening of his attitude, he turned aside from her, saying harshly: 'She's probably humouring you for some reason of her own,' and Joanna's temper exploded into action.

'You won't listen to reason, will you?' she exclaimed, brushing past him, and in her haste her breasts bounced against the firm muscle of his arm.

She didn't know which of them was the most affected by the incident. She was aware of Jake drawing aside from her, his face tense and guarded, and of the tingling sensation she was still feeling from that disturbing contact. It was strange because she had had far more familiar contacts with young men of her own age, occasions when she had been on holiday in the south of France, and had attended beach barbecues wearing only a bikini, and danced the night away; yet just by brushing Jake's arm with her breasts she was made more intimately aware of his masculinity than with any other man she had ever met.

She was still standing there, arms crossed over her body, palms massaging her elbows, when Anya came into the kitchen, and it was lucky that her delight in seeing her father distracted her awareness of the tense attitudes of the other two people in the room. She came towards Jake eagerly, and Joanna quickly applied herself to the teacups, hardly conscious of anything except a sense of blind impotence. He was sending her away, she thought bitterly, and if there had been any doubts in his mind, she had probably destroyed them by her unthinking provocation.

'Did Miss Seton tell you what we've been doing today?' Anya asked, blithely indifferent to her father's bleak countenance, and while Joanna waited with bated breath for the girl to tell Jake about her writing, she added: 'We cleared out the library.' She arched her brows as if expecting dispute. 'Honestly! It was awfully dusty. Miss Seton said you could practically grow mushrooms behind the bookshelves!'

Joanna's shoulders sagged, and she was hardly surprised when Jake expressed no enthusiasm for the project. 'As I persistently keep having to remind Miss Seton, she was brought here to supervise your studies, not to act as an unpaid domestic,' he retorted brusquely, but this time Anya made no mistake.

'But she is, Daddy,' she protested, casting an appealing look in Joanna's direction. 'We did the cleaning this morning. This afternoon we've done school work.'

Jake's mouth compressed. 'Is this true?' he demanded, and Joanna met the narrow-eyed gaze he turned upon her with grim determination.

'I did try to tell you,' she said, annoyed to hear the tremor in her voice, and he turned back to his daughter in reluctant contrition.

'And what did Miss Seton have to say about your work?' he enquired distantly. 'Did she find your general abilities as sadly limited as her predecessor?'

'No!' It was Joanna who spoke, interjecting her own response before Anya could say anything. She didn't like his manner of interrogation, slanted as it was towards corrupting the tenuous understanding she and his daughter were achieving, and if she hadn't known he had Anya's well-being at heart, she would have said he was doing his best to turn the child against her. But why? Why? There was no time now to explore such a notion, and she went on quickly: 'Anya's capabilities are not limited. She—she's an intelligent child. A sensitive child,' she added forcefully. 'And she has a genuine aptitude for English.'

He was obliged to look at her again then. 'For story-writing, don't you mean, Miss Seton?' he suggested coldly.

'An over-active imagination, which it sounds as though you are encouraging.'

'I am.' Joanna disliked having to argue with him in front of the child, but there was no other way. 'Why not? Her stories are good! Her grasp of description is outstanding for a girl of her age.'

Jake's hard eyes bored into hers, and the silent battle of wills it instigated was something Joanna knew she had to win. But not at the expense of Anya's peace of mind, and aware of the child's gaze upon them, she said deliberately:

'I know you don't like me, Mr Sheldon. You've made that very clear. But I think in this instance it's more important that Anya take advantage of the little I can teach her than that you and I should allow our personal differences to interfere with her future.'

It was a consummate piece of acting, considering the chaotic turmoil of her emotions, and one he could hardly gainsay. It served the dual purpose of diverting Anya's attention from their growing familiarity with one another, and at the same time left him little room for manoeuvre without arousing her suspicions.

'Very well,' he said at last, expelling his breath on a heavy sigh. 'Since you seem at least to have won her confidence, I have no choice but to submit to the reason of your argument. However, I will defer any decision on the matter for the present time. Unless I can find a suitable woman to come and take charge of Ravengarth, I may be forced to make other arrangements.'

What those other arrangements might be Joanna had no idea, and Anya was only concerned with her own affairs anyway.

'Miss Seton's pretty good at housekeeping,' she volunteered thoughtfully. 'Couldn't you pay her twice as much to do both jobs?'

'No.' Jake's response was clipped. 'Somehow I've got to find a woman who's prepared to put up with the isolation of Ravengarth in exchange for a good salary, and until I do, I'm making no promises.'

It was not a satisfactory answer, but Joanna had to accept

it. At least, he was not dismissing her out of hand, she thought weakly, and then wondered if it wouldn't have been better if he had. Staying here, she sensed she was inviting trouble of a kind she had not yet experienced, but nothing would have induced her to leave. In some strange, incomprehensible way, she was involved with the scarred master of Ravengarth, and for good or ill she had chosen her own fate.

CHAPTER SEVEN

DURING the next few days Joanna had little time to worry about the expediency of her decision. Despite Jake's objections to her taking over the household, there was no one else to do it, and it was amazing how quickly she adapted to her new life. She made mistakes, the rarefied existence she had lived before coming to Ravengarth ill preparing her for the everyday obstacles that were thrown in her path, but apart from scorching one of the sheets by putting it too close to the fire, and breaking some of the china from the cabinet in the living room when she tried to wash it in water that was too hot, she felt she was succeeding reasonably well.

Certainly Anya did not protest at her prolonged spells of housekeeping, but this was because it meant there was less time for lessons. Anya, she had discovered, did not work well without supervision, but she joined Joanna in her spurts of cleaning with real enthusiasm, and she guessed the little girl's latent femininity was being stimulated by so much activity. It was obvious that Mrs Harris had more to answer for than just poor housekeeping, and Joanna fumed every time she thought of her baulking the child's natural development.

Jake himself kept mostly out of the way. Even at meal times, he endeavoured to appear after they had finished, and although he ate the food Joanna put before him, she always had the feeling he would rather have had dry bread. In this respect it was an unsatisfactory situation, but in no other. She closed her mind to the realisation that it was her he was avoiding, and told herself that once he acquired a suitable housekeeper, he would have to recognise what she was doing for his daughter.

So far as Anya was concerned, Joanna's ingenuity amazed her. Quite by chance really, she had discovered how to engage the girl's attention, and by involving the practical as well as the academic methods of teaching, she had aroused Anya's interest.

It was astonishingly easy, once she had learned how to turn the situation to her advantage. Anya responded to anything that remotely involved the stories she told so avidly, and as soon as Joanna detected this she used it to good effect. Those first intimations of how history and geography could help her developed through Joanna's patient instruction into a genuine interest in both, and gradually it became apparent that Anya was good at anything she really applied herself to. The area around Ravengarth was ideal for their purpose. It was rich in history, for one thing, a blending of Roman remains and nineteenth-century industry, and its lakes and mountains, springs and rock formations were a living indication of the developing geography of northern England. That Joanna's teaching took in science and geology as well was not important; what was important was that Anya was beginning to find the pursuit of knowledge challenging. The secret was to keep it entertaining, and Joanna discovered a quite unexpected ability to achieve this. If Anya was learning to enjoy lessons, Joanna was learning about herself, and the knowledge was amazingly satisfying.

She had written to her mother, assuring her that she had settled down at Ravengarth, but without going into much detail about the actual circumstances of her employment. She had merely let her mother assume that there was nothing unusual about the situation, implying a household adequately supervised, where she was actively employed in her capacity as governess. Without actually coming to Ravengarth, no one would be any the wiser, and Jake's sister would no doubt reassure both Joanna's mother and her godmother that it seemed to have turned out well for all concerned.

Paul Trevor appeared unexpectedly one morning almost a week after Joanna's visit to his parents' farm. He came in the Land Rover, parking in the yard much to the indignation of the dogs, who set up their barking, and Joanna came out to see what all the noise was about. She had not expected a visitor, and as Jake had gone to Penrith, ostensibly for some supplies, she had taken the opportunity to spring-clean the living room. Already the house was beginning to show the results of her management, and where once there had been dust and grime now there was the sweet smell of beeswax.

It meant, however, that she was wearing her oldest pair of jeans, a cotton shirt that hung loosely outside her pants, and a scarf knotted round her head, hiding the silken abundance of her hair. She was immediately conscious of this as Paul came strolling across the yard towards her, and her colour rose as he stretched out a provocative finger and wiped a speck of soot from her nose.

'Hi there,' he said, his square handsome face creased into a smile. 'You look as though you're busy. Could it be that you're teaching chimney-sweeping as part of the curriculum?'

Joanna sighed. 'I'm cleaning, actually,' she said, feeling obliged to invite him into the kitchen. 'This is a surprise, Paul. You should have let me know you were coming.'

His expression grew a little wry at this, and with a shrug he answered: 'I didn't think Sheldon would appreciate me coming over when he was around, and when I heard old Coulston telling George at the pub that he was going to Penrith this morning, I decided this was my opportunity.'

'I see.' Joanna glanced round. 'Well—er—can I offer you a drink? Some coffee, perhaps? I was just about to have one myself.'

'I'd love a cup of coffee,' Paul agreed, though his expression was more perplexed than anything when Joanna filled the kettle. 'But where's Mrs Harris? Couldn't she do that for you? Or is she cleaning, too?'

Joanna sighed, realising that she couldn't evade his questions here as she had done at the Trevors. 'Mrs Harris has left,' she said, setting cups on a tray as she spoke. 'Mr Sheldon is looking for a new housekeeper, but until he does——'

'You're not looking after this place, are you?' Paul interrupted her in an appalled voice. 'My God! What a bloody nerve that man has! What does he think you are? Some kind of menial or something?'

'Oh, please ...' Joanna glanced apprehensively towards the hall door. Anya was in the library, reading an article about artesian wells Joanna had discovered in one of the science magazines she had found in the living room, and the last thing she wanted was for the child to imagine she was dissatisfied with the situation. 'I offered to help until someone else could be found. I don't mind, honestly.'

'But this place is too big for one person to handle!' he protested, and she sighed again.

'We don't use all the rooms,' she explained. 'Just a bedroom each, the library, and the sitting room. We eat in here. It's easier.'

'But you—you're not used to this,' Paul objected, pulling out a chair from the table and sitting down rather unwillingly. 'I mean, it's obvious you've been used to a different kind of life ...'

Joanna smiled then. 'Is it so obvious?' she exclaimed dryly. 'That's no compliment. I don't think I like the idea of being regarded as completely useless.'

'I didn't mean that.' Paul was vehement in his protest. 'Joanna——'

'I was only teasing,' she assured him, and turned away to put instant coffee into two earthenware beakers. 'There you are,' she added boiling water to the cup and handed it to him. 'There's cream on the table, and sugar too, if you need it. Help yourself.'

Paul did so, and after taking a mouthful of his coffee, put the cup down and fumbled in his pocket for a handful of notes and silver. 'This is yours,' he said, counting it out carefully. 'The change from those notes you gave to me. I'd hate you to think I'd forgotten it.'

Joanna shook her head. 'I wouldn't think a thing like that, Paul. But thank you, anyway. I was very grateful.'

'Any time,' he assured her fervently, his eyes on her face revealing the warmth of his feelings. 'But now that's out of the way, there's something I wanted to ask you. Will you have a meal with me one evening? In Penrith, or Keswick. I could pick you up here about seven, and we could drive——'

'I'm afraid that's not possible at the moment.' Joanna had no particular desire to go out with Paul at all. He was a pleasant young man, and she liked him, but she had no intention of getting involved with him. Still, she had to be tactful, and making an apologetic gesture she added: 'Someone has to be here to look after Anya, and until Ja— Mr Sheldon gets someone else——'

If Paul noticed the slip, he showed no reaction to it, but it gave Joanna quite a shock to realise that that was how she thought of her employer. However, Paul's next words distracted her attention, and she listened to him doubtfully as he offered a solution.

'Why doesn't he ask in the village?' Paul suggested rather impatiently. 'I happen to know there are one or two widows who could do with a supplement to their income, and they'd probably be willing to work here now that Mrs Harris has gone.'

Joanna's brow puckered. 'They didn't like Mrs Harris?'

'Hell no.' Paul grimaced at his language. 'They never forgave her for what she did to Mrs Fawcett, and so long as she was at Ravengarth ...' He shrugged. 'I could ask around.'

'Would you?' Joanna's spirits rose.

Paul hesitated. 'If I do, will you promise to have dinner with me if I succeed?'

Joanna stalled. 'Won't someone from the village want to go home in the evenings?'

Paul frowned. 'You have a point. It's not really a suitable arrangement, is it? You living here alone with Sheldon, and only a child as chaperone.'

'I didn't mean that.' Joanna flushed. The last thing she wanted was to promote that kind of speculation. 'I just meant—if this person, whoever she is, does go home in the evenings, she won't be on hand to look after Anya.'

'You could ask her,' Paul remarked dryly. 'Well, what do you say?'

Joanna pressed her lips together. 'So long as Mr Sheldon doesn't object,' she said at last.

'Why should be?' Paul was indignant. 'From what I hear, he doesn't give a damn about anybody but himself.'

'That's not true!' Joanna couldn't prevent the outburst.

'That's not my opinion. Living here like a recluse, never meeting his neighbours, never accepting invitations or giving them. Just because he was cut up in that car crash it doesn't mean he has to cut himself off from other people. What's the matter? Aren't we good enough for him?'

So that was it. Joanna now understood Mrs Trevor's attitude when they were first introduced. Did it also explain why the villagers regarded Jake as eccentric? And if Mrs Harris had been the reason why none of them would work at Ravengarth, then Jake's selfconsciousness about his appearance was unfounded.

Anya chose that moment to put in her appearance, which was just as well, as Joanna had no desire to discuss her employer in personal terms. She came sauntering into the kitchen, and regarded Paul without hostility before turning her gaze to Joanna. She looked much different from the ragged urchin she had first encountered, Joanna thought with satisfaction, and although she still wore jeans and a sweater, they were clean and tidy, and her dark hair was smoothly brushed.

'Can I have some coffee, Joanna?' she asked, darting another glance at Paul as she did so. Joanna had given her permission to use her Christian name whenever they were alone together, but this was the first time she had used it in front of anyone else. It made Paul arch his brows in mild disapproval of the familiarity, and Joanna wondered if the lapse had been deliberate.

'You don't like coffee,' she said now, and the girl pulled a wry face.

'Some milk, then,' she said, shrugging her thin shoulders, and Joanna guessed she just wanted a reason to find out what was going on.

'Did you finish the article?' Joanna asked, pouring milk

into a glass, and Anya nodded.

'I read another article, too, about whales,' she exclaimed, diverted for a moment. 'Did you know they were an—en-endangered spe-species?'

'Some,' Joanna admitted gently, touched by her concern. 'I'm glad you found it so interesting. Perhaps we should incorporate biology into our studies, too.'

'Biology?' Anya frowned. 'What's that?'

'It's the study of animals and plants,' Paul answered her shortly, not at all pleased at this unwelcome intrusion to his conversation with Joanna. 'Look, I'd better be going, Joanna. I'll let you know what luck I have as soon as possible.'

'What is he going to let you know about?' asked Anya curiously, but Paul only gave her an impatient stare.

'Probably tomorrow,' he said, continuing his thread. 'How about coming down to the pub tomorrow evening for a drink? We could talk it over.'

Anya was wide-eyed by now, and Joanna felt a little irritated by his persistence. 'I think it would be better if you let us know if you have any success,' she declared firmly. 'I'm sure Mr Sheldon would appreciate it.'

Paul shrugged, but he had to accept her decision. However, after he had gone Joanna still had Anya to contend with.

'He fancies you, doesn't he?' she remarked slyly, and Joanna guessed the terms were Mrs Harris's, not hers.

'Mr Trevor is going to try and find a housekeeper for us,' she replied flatly. 'That's all. Now, you can help me carry the china out of the cabinet in the living room. I want to wash it before I put it back.'

'Daddy won't like that,' observed Anya sagely, accompanying her through the door, and Joanna felt the familiar pangs of frustration.

'Why not?' she argued, despising herself for doing so, and Anya grimaced as she offered her opinion.

'We don't get involved with the people around here,' she said, experimentally snapping her fingers. 'And you know how angry he was when he found you were at the Trevors'.

I don't think he'll be very pleased at you asking that man to find someone to work here.'

Joanna felt her temper simmering, and knew it was because Anya was saying all the things she herself had suspected and determinedly squashed. 'I didn't *ask* him,' she replied now, jerking open the door of the cupboard and almost dislodging a piece of Wedgwood. 'He offered. And I should have thought your father would be only too relieved to think that his problems might soon be over.'

Anya shrugged. 'You'll see,' she said, with an annoying smirk, and for the first time for days Joanna could have willingly slapped her.

As it happened, Joanna was not around when Jake returned. After cleaning out the cupboards and restoring polish to the floor surrounding the worn carpet, she had decided to wash the curtains, only to discover they were out of soap powder. The generous amount of washing she had done in the last few days had exhausted their supply, and it was something she had forgotten to put on the list Jake had taken with him. Some time, she hoped he would invite her to accompany him on one of his trips to the town, but she doubted it would happen in the near future. There was an alternative, of course. She could ask to borrow the Range Rover and drive herself, and as she intended to discuss Anya's wardrobe in the not-too-distant future, she was hoping to persuade him to allow her to take the girl with her.

For the present, however, only the village store could supply her needs, and as Anya seemed quite happy to continue looking through the science magazines, she walked to Ravensmere alone. This time she made no mistake in the directions Matt had given her, and she eventually came down the lane into the village feeling reasonably pleased with her efforts.

The village store was a comprehensive one, encompassing a post office as well as a greengrocers and general dealers. Because of the demands of tourists in the area, it was quite well equipped, and Joanna carried her basket round the adequately stocked shelves with an unusual feeling of independence. Since leaving London she had not entered a shop of any kind, and she realised how much she had missed it.

The girl at the till she guessed to be the daughter of the owner of the store, and she stared at Joanna rather curiously as she unloaded her shopping beside the small checkout. Joanna passed the time of day with her, but refused to be drawn into conversation after Anya's gloomy forecast of Jake's reactions. However, she emerged from the store aware that she had been very thoroughly inspected. She surmised that Paul had told them about her presence at Ravengarth, and as there were few visitors in the area at this time of year, she could hardly be expected to keep her identity a secret.

She was crossing the main street on her way back to Ravengarth when a dark green vehicle braked to a halt beside her. She glanced round carelessly, imagining it to be a delivery van, and then halted uncertainly as she encountered Jake's hard unyielding features.

'Get in,' he commanded, thrusting open the door of the Range Rover from the inside, and with a helpless shrug she complied, not altogether sorry to be relieved of the unaccustomed weight of her shopping bag.

Jake waited until she had closed the door behind her, and then put the vehicle into gear, setting away rather aggressively. The tires spun on the slightly damp road, but Joanna, noticing his set face, refrained from saying anything which might aggravate an already volatile situation. She didn't know whether he had encountered her by accident or design, but either way he was not pleased, and she waited in slightly nervous anticipation for him to speak.

'I thought I made it clear that I do not wish you to shop in the village,' he said at last, his voice harshly controlled. 'It seems you take a delight in doing those things I ask you not to do, and I do not intend to be made a fool of by a girl little older than my own daughter.'

'I'm not making a fool of you,' she protested, turning to look at him. 'I needed some soap powder, so I came to get some. Why shouldn't I? I'm not a prisoner. I do need some freedom. Just because you have some mistaken idea that people care——'

'We won't discuss it,' he overrode her brusquely. 'So long as you're in my employ, you will confine your shopping expeditions to Penrith or Keswick, and as we're on the subject, it is not part of your duties to do the washing.'

'Then who is to do it?' Joanna retorted, incensed by his inflexibility, but he merely shrugged.

'There's a laundromat in Penrith——'

'Laundromats are not for garments that need careful attention.'

His mouth hardened. 'And do the living room curtains need careful attention?'

Joanna hunched her shoulders. 'You've been home.' It was a statement, not a question, and he inclined his head.

'As you say.'

'And Anya told you where I was?'

'As I wanted to visit the vet at Heronsfoot, it was only a short detour.'

Joanna glanced quickly through the windows and realised that in her anxiety she had not noticed they were not on their way back to the house. So he was taking her with him, she thought, trying to be offhand about it, but her churning stomach refused to respond.

'Where is Anya anyway?' she asked, concerned what she might get up to without supervision, but Jake had taken control.

'She's all right. I left her helping Matt build a bonfire,' he retorted, and she breathed a sigh of relief that she had this short respite.

'Besides,' he added shortly, 'I wanted to talk to you, and now seemed as good a time as any.'

Joanna sighed, her elation at this unexpected outing evaporating somewhat. 'I know. You want to express your objections to me cleaning the house.'

'That, of course,' he retorted curtly, 'but there is another matter which has to be disposed of—this penchant you have for interfering in affairs that don't concern you.'

'What?'

Joanna was confused, and he turned his cold amber eyes in her direction. 'Don't pretend you don't understand, Miss Seton. Anya has told me about young Trevor's visit this morning, and some arrangement you have with him if he succeeds in finding a woman to work at Ravengarth!'

Joanna gasped. She might have known that Anya would not let such a heavensent opportunity escape her, and while it was not unreasonable that she should have told her father about the housekeeper, it was obvious she had been listening at the door long before she chose to make her entrance. How else could she have known about the bargain Paul had suggested? He had certainly not repeated it in her hearing.

'Paul offered to ask one or two people in the village whether they would consider working at Ravengarth, that's all,' she declared tersely. 'I think it was kind of him. After all, you've had no luck in obtaining a housekeeper, and at least if one of the village women does come to work for you, she won't be requiring accommodation.'

Jake turned to look at her once again. 'And you think that is a recommendation?' he asked bleakly. 'Are you not aware of the talk there'll be in the village right this moment, now they know Mrs Harris has departed?'

Joanna's face burned. 'Does it matter?' she exclaimed, unable to sustain his searching gaze. 'As you persistently point out, I am young enough to be your daughter!'

'But you're not my daughter,' he snapped, forced to halt as they reached the sliproad on to the motorway. 'And the longer you remain at Ravengarth, the more convinced I become that your staying is a mistake.'

Joanna sank back in her seat as if he had struck her. It was obvious, he was only keeping her on because of the minor success she was having with Anya, and she guessed that if he could find some older woman to do the job she was doing she would be dismissed, just like Mrs Harris. It was a daunting thought, and it successfully destroyed what little exhilaration was left to her. She remained silent during the remainder of the journey to Heronsfoot, and stayed in the Range Rover while he went into the vet's. What was the point of getting involved? she asked herself bitterly; he was determined to maintain the barrier of detachment with her, just as he did with everyone else.

He wasn't long, and presently he came striding back to the vehicle, tall and disruptively masculine in his black leather jacket and corded pants. His shirt, one of the coarse grey shirts she herself had washed and ironed, was open at the throat, exposing the strong column of his neck, and with the breeze ruffling the smooth dark hair, he looked dark and disturbing.

His eyes met hers as he pulled open his door and got inside, levering his long length behind the wheel. For a heart-stopping moment they looked at one another without either fear or aggression, and Joanna's lips parted on an involuntary breath. She didn't want to break that unguarded contact, and it was Jake who leant forward and deliberately started the engine before she could say anything.

Heronsfoot was a village similar to Ravensmere, but as it was just off the motorway it was considerably busier. There were several shops and a café Joanna had seen as they drove through, and now, hardly aware of what she was saying, she used them as a delaying tactic.

'Is—is there a pharmacy here?' she exclaimed, as he swung away from the curb, and heard the sudden intake of his breath as he was obliged to answer her.

'There's a chemists,' he amended shortly. 'Why? Is there something else you want?'

'Yes.' Joanna thought furiously. 'I—er—I need some nail varnish remover.'

'Nail varnish remover?' Jake applied his brakes reluctantly. 'Can't it wait?'

'Until when?' she enquired ironically. 'You've just told me I mustn't shop in Ravensmere.'

His lips thinned, but he pulled into the curb again, and indicated the small leaded-paned shop window opposite. 'Don't be long,' he advised, with an impatient gesture, and grateful for the reprieve, she pushed open her door, deliberately leaving her purse behind.

The chemist was a young man, and he smiled under-

standingly when she confessed that she had left her money
in the car. It wasn't every day he had such an attractive
young woman in his shop, and he watched the unconscious
swing of her hips as Joanna sauntered across the road again
and tapped on Jake's window.

'I've forgotten my purse,' she said innocently, as he
wound the window down. 'Could you possibly come and
pay for it for me? It will save me having to unpack all those
things.' She pointed to the shopping bag on the back seat
of the vehicle.

Jake hesitated, looked as though he was going to object,
and then thrust open his door. Joanna watched him tri-
umphantly, then turned and walked back to the shop with
him following. She was well aware of the café only two
doors further along, but when they emerged from the
chemist a few moments later she pretended a spontaneous
exclamation.

'Would you mind if we had a cup of tea before going
back?' she asked, depending on that unguarded moment to
win the day, and was bitterly disappointed when he strode
across the road.

'If you want a cup of tea, get it,' he advised shortly. 'I'll
wait for you in the Rover, but don't be long.'

Joanna pursed her lips. 'I don't have any money.'

'Then you'll have to do without, won't you?' he retorted,
evidently deducing what she had had in mind, and with a
feeling of impotence she came back to the car.

'I wanted to talk to you,' she said half sulkily, as he
pulled away, but Jake did not immediately answer her. He
drove in silence until they were clear of the small town,
and then he said harshly:

'I do not like being made a fool of, Miss Seton.'

Joanna flushed. 'That wasn't my intention.'

'No?' He glanced sideways at her. 'But you didn't really
want to go to the chemists, did you? Your real objective
was the café. I should tell you, I do not take tea in cafés,
unless it's unavoidable.'

Joanna sighed. 'If you're about to tell me your appearance is responsible——' she began, and then broke off in

dismay when he brought the Range Rover to an abrupt halt.

'We will have no psycho-analysing here, Miss Seton,' he snapped savagely, turning in his seat so that the heat of his breath was tangible against her temple. He made an impatient gesture before continuing: 'I thought I knew why you came here. I believed what my sister told me. But it becomes more and more apparent that you're not satisfied to simply get on with the job for which you were employed. I concede that you've had some small success with Anya, and for this reason I've tried to be tolerant, but I will not permit the kind of familiarity between us you seem bent on promoting.'

Joanna stared at him, at once aghast and resentful of his perception. 'I don't know what you're talking about,' she muttered, her lower lip jutting. 'Just because I forgot my purse and you had to help me ...'

'You didn't forget your purse,' retorted Jake coldly, reaching round into the back and extracting the offending article from the top of her shopping bag. 'It was a little trick to get me out of the car. Well, you succeeded, but that's all. Do you understand?'

Joanna held up her head. 'When I came here, Mr Sheldon, you talked of me being too—imaginative; has it occurred to you that you might be the imaginative one, not me?'

Jake's mouth hardened perceptibly, and the air around them moistened and condensed on the windows. The fast-misting panes enclosed them in an atmosphere of isolation that was almost claustrophobic, Joanna felt, cutting down her surroundings to the leather-seated interior of the car, her vision to the scarred lean face of the man beside her.

'You invite violence, do you know that?' he snapped, tugging angrily at the hair at the back of his neck. 'You're not dealing with some youth, enamoured by the flattery of your interest! You and I have to work with one another, that's all. Anything else is out of the question.'

Joanna was astounded now, as much by his effrontery as by her reactions to it. 'You have no grounds for making such an outrageous statement!' she protested incredulously. 'Just because I'm trying to create the kind of situation where we might—*discuss* matters that affect us both——'

'Like Trevor finding a housekeeper for us, you mean?' Jake overrode her coldly, and she pressed her lips together.

'I've told you. Paul had your best interests at heart——'

'Yours, you mean,' he corrected her bleakly. 'I may be disfigured, but my eyes are as good as anyone else's. I know why—*Paul* is suddenly so helpful, and it has nothing to do with me or Anya.'

Joanna was incensed. 'Jealous, Mr Sheldon?' she jeered, unable to hide the derision in her voice, only to freeze into immobility when his hands imprisoned her shoulders, pressing her back against the dark green leather of the upholstery. He was much closer now, only the length of an arm away, and a bent arm at that. The tawny amber eyes held her frozen gaze with the expertise of the snake with the rabbit, and her heart seemed suspended by the expression in their depths.

'This is the moment you've been waiting for, isn't it?' he said suddenly, and she realised in dismay that he was taunting her now. 'We've all seen those old movies, haven't we? The heroine mocks the hero one time too many, and he responds in the age-old way of all heroes.' His lips twisted. 'Only I'm no hero, Miss Seton, and I fear you're not the stuff of which heroines are made either. You're trembling—I can feel it. Why? Isn't a little romantic diversion what you're missing? Isn't that the reason why I'm being flattered by all this unwarranted attention?'

It was awful, but she could think of nothing to say in her own defence. 'You—you're a brute!' she got out chokingly. 'Let go of me! You have no right to treat me like this. How many times must I tell you, I only wanted to talk!'

His narrow-eyed gaze held hers for a moment longer, grew speculative, then pensive, and finally moved down over the delicate planes of her face to the vulnerable uncertainty of her mouth. And she was vulnerable, she realised with a pang. Weak, and vulnerable, and pathetically in-

experienced. The young men she had known had not prepared her for the complexities of Jake's character, and her
little charade seemed puerile in the face of his denunciation.

'What did Marcia tell you about me?' he demanded
roughly, making no move to release her. 'What manner of
man did she say I was? I suppose she told you about Beth,
and the accident—and why I'm living the life of a country
yokel?'

'She didn't—that is—I don't know your sister,' protested
Joanna desperately. 'It was Aunt Lydia who—arranged
everything.'

'Lady Sutton?'

'Yes.'

Jake's eyes narrowed in disbelief. 'But you've heard
about my wife, haven't you? And the reasons why I left
London.'

'Mr Sheldon, I don't think——'

'What don't you think?' he overrode her a little cruelly.
'That it has anything to do with you? No, I'd agree with
you, it hasn't. But you're here—and perhaps I feel the need
to talk to someone.'

Joanna wished she'd never started this. 'Mr Sheldon——'

'I was an engineer, you know,' he remarked, almost as if
he was talking to himself. 'In electronics, the career of the
future. That is where the future lies, you know, in electronics. Silicon chips!' His lips twisted. 'But I won't be a
part of it.'

Joanna shifted nervously beneath his numbing grasp.
She had the feeling that by her reckless behaviour she had
triggered off some morbid introspection, that could only
bring pain and bitterness to him, but she didn't know how
to reverse the process.

'Why?' she asked now, searching for a means to reassure
him, and the harsh mouth twisted in unwilling recollection.

'It was the accident, you see,' he went on, in that flat
monotone. 'Afterwards, I couldn't concentrate on anything,
not without getting this God-awful pain in my head. It was
hopeless. When I tried to work, I couldn't. The simplest
calculations were beyond me. Resistors, transistors, micro-

processors; my brain just couldn't absorb the information. I'd lost the ability to work effectively.' He shook his head. 'I guess you could say these scars were a godsend. At least they gave me an excuse to get out of London, to lick my wounds in private.'

'So you bought Ravengarth?'

Joanna wondered if he was really aware of how painful his grip on her shoulder was, but her words were more honestly an attempt to divert his anger until she could wriggle out of his grasp.

'Yes,' he said, his thumb probing the narrow bones of her shoulder through the thickness of her jacket. 'I'd always enjoyed painting as a hobby, and I thought I might enjoy the rustic life. I knew I had to do something or go mad, and a smallholding like Ravengarth seemed the most sensible idea. Unfortunately, it hasn't worked out as I expected.' His brows descended, and she realised he was remembering her behaviour again. 'Not as I expected at all.'

'Don't you think we ought to be going back?' she ventured, hoping that now he had unburdened himself he might be more willing to respond to her suggestion, but all it brought was a deepening of his brooding gaze.

'That was not what you had in mind earlier,' he pointed out tormentingly. 'Surely I'm not scaring you, Miss Seton? Surely, after all you've said about this face, it hasn't suddenly begun to frighten you.'

Joanna pressed her lips together. 'Your face has nothing to do with it,' she exclaimed tautly. 'I've told you before, you've lived with it too long. It's not repulsive—not repulsive at all.'

'So if I put it close to yours—like this,' he came nearer until she could see every pore of his dark flesh, every ridge of scar tissue, every betraying spasm as the muscles tightened in his jaw, 'you wouldn't draw back from me?'

'No!'

But she did. Not through any revulsion against his appearance, rather because his nearness frightened her in other ways, ways she hardly understood, but which left her

weak with the awareness that she had to restrain herself
from touching him.

'Liar!' Clearly he had misunderstood her involuntary
withdrawal, and his face contorted with contempt. 'You
can't bear to be this close to me, can you? It screws you
up. Well, let's see how you react to a more physical demonstration . . .' and lowering his head, he found her mouth
with his.

Joanna's lips were already parted in protest, and his unexpected assault found no opposition. At the touch of those
firm lips, her resistance faltered, and he only needed that
involuntary submission to succeed in his intent. She was
already far too aware of the muscled strength of his body,
and his weight crushing her back against the seat was itself a potent intoxicant. She had unbuttoned her coat in the
warmth of the car, and his chest was hard against the thinly
protected fullness of her breasts. It didn't help to know
that they were swollen and hardened against his broad
chest, responding without her consent to the demanding
pressure of his body.

But it was his mouth which wrought the most damage,
invading and possessing the moist sweetness of hers. What
had begun as an attempt to discourage her deepened into
a passionate possession, and his hands which only minutes
before had been bruising the bones of her shoulders were
now probing the small of her back, gripping her narrow
waist, sliding under the hem of her shirt to find the pointed
nipples eager for his exploration.

Her half-hearted attempts to deter him were met with
resistance, and besides, she was invaded by an unfamiliar
weakness in her thighs as his hard fingers continued the
sinuous massage. She was glad she was not wearing a bra
that afternoon, and she surged against him inviting his un-
restrained caress.

His mouth descended in a burning trail of kisses from
her lips to her nape, and her hands groped for him, for
the lapels of his jacket, like a drowning man groping for a
lifeline. It was an instinctive response to his sensuous viola-

tion, and almost unaware her fingers probed the taut muscles of his thigh.

His withdrawal was as unexpected as the devastating effect he had had on her. One minute his mouth was stroking hers, moving sensually upon it, teaching her how little she had known of her own emotions, and the next she was thrust away from him, her tentative fingers arrested in their search, his breath expelling from his lips in a mutter of self-revulsion. With a savage oath he rested his elbows on the steering wheel, pushing back the thickness of his hair with both hands, his dark face twisted into an expression of self disgust.

'*My God!*' The words were wrung from him, harsh and contemptuous in that charged atmosphere. 'What the hell am I doing? Letting you provoke me like this! I must be out of mind!'

Joanna didn't know what to say, what to do. She felt helpless against the storm of emotion he had aroused inside her, and dazed by her response to the ruthless arrogance of his assault. It was both troubling and humiliating to know that he had torn down every defence she raised against him, leaving her shocked and exposed to the raw brutality of his verbal attack.

'I don't think there's any point in conducting a post-mortem,' she got out at last, unsteadily, smoothing her hair with shaking fingers, and he turned violent eyes in her direction.

'You don't?' There was cold sarcasm in his tone.

'No.' Joanna endeavoured to compose her defence. 'It— I—what happened—happened. It's not something——'

'You invited it, is that it?' he demanded savagely, and she caught her breath.

'No——'

'But you did, Miss Seton. You're a provoking person. I knew that the first time I laid eyes on you.'

'So why did you keep me, then?' she cried, stung by his coldness after the interlude they had just shared. 'Why didn't you just tell me I wasn't suitable, instead of letting me stay under false pretences?'

'Beggars can't be choosers, Miss Seton,' he responded, bleakly. 'A trite saying, but true. And now, I think, we ought to be getting back. Until other arrangements can be made, you will continue as Anya's governess, but that's all. You'll be happy to know, I'm sure,' the sarcasm was back now, 'that I was successful at last in finding a house-keeper——'

'Did Paul——' she began, her face brightening slightly, but he killed her anticipation with a hard smile.

'On my own merits, Miss Seton. From the agency in Penrith. I told you, I didn't need anyone's assistance. Mrs Parrish arrives tomorrow. Perhaps that will help to scotch any rumours about our relationship which your friends the Trevors may have promoted, and also terminate your amateur attempts at housekeeping!'

CHAPTER EIGHT

IT was easy to sustain her anger against him, but not so easy to dispel the urgent awakening of feelings he had incited. Her resentment at his arrogance was genuine enough, but it hurt to know that while she had been overwhelmed by emotions stronger than any she had ever known, Jake had been merely expunging his frustration. Since his wife's death, he had been denied any physical relationship with a woman, and for a brief moment she had supplied a need. But it was not a need he welcomed or enjoyed. His reactions afterwards had made that plain enough, and she found herself wondering about the kind of relationship he had had with his wife, and how she would have reacted to this harsh, embittered individual who must bear little resemblance to the man he had once been.

Mrs Parrish arrived, as expected, the following afternoon. She came from Penrith, driving her own small car, and Joanna watched from the library window as Jake went to greet her. She was a small woman, brown-haired and dark-eyed, and Anya, who had been free to question her father, had told her that she was a widow with a grown-up family. Certainly her appearance alone was a far cry from Mrs Harris's slovenly ways, and in the following days Joanna's respect for her abilities increased. She was obviously quite capable of running the house single-handed, and although she missed the sense of satisfaction she had gained organising the household, Joanna much appreciated the good food she was served, and the absence of the neglect which had so characterised Ravengarth on her arrival.

Mrs Parrish was not a gossip either. If she found the situation at Ravengarth intriguing, she refrained from saying so, merely confining her comments to a sincere sympathy for someone who had lost so much so quickly. To Joanna, these remarks had a double-edged sting, and although she conceded that Jake bore his burden well, she found her own sympathies much divided. Jake's attitude was not one of a man bereft, and she suspected his belief in his own incapacity had never been put to the test. With Anya's increasing interest in her school work, he was often called upon to examine her efforts, and his reactions were not those of someone unable to grasp the problems she showed him. Joanna wished she knew more about these matters, but she was beginning to believe that Jake's disabilities had been temporary, a consequence of the accident, no more, and given the opportunity, his brain would respond to any kind of stimulus.

Not that she could say such a thing to him. Since that scene in the Range Rover he had avoided her like the plague, and every exchange they had had, had been in the company of either Anya or Mrs Parrish. There had been no more talk of her leaving, and she guessed that so long as she kept her place and Anya appeared happy, there would not be, and at times she was tempted to try a little brinkmanship on her own account. But the idea of leaving Ravengarth had become so abhorrent to her that she remained in that state of limbo he had created, and determinedly ignored the ambiguity of the situation.

She managed to persuade Anya that some new clothes would not come amiss, particularly as with the advent of October the weather had turned much colder. Mrs Parrish had succeeded in turning on the ancient heating system without blowing up the boiler, but the radiators were few and hardly adequate, and until the fires were lit it was necessary to wear something warm. In consequence, Joanna approached Jake one morning with the request that she might borrow the Range Rover and take Anya into Penrith.

Jake was in the barn when she found him, forking fresh hay into the stall where Gertrude came for milking, and for once Matt wasn't with him. Between them the two men did all the jobs about the holding, which included looking after the score or so of sheep, feeding the chickens, milking the cow, and all the other duties necessary to the efficient running of the place. Joanna had not yet discovered how Jake found the time to do any painting, and certainly in the three weeks since her arrival he had avoided spending long periods in the house.

Now he looked up warily at her approach, and his mouth took on a downward slant when he saw that she was alone.

'Yes?'

The enquiry was short, and Joanna couldn't deny the twinge of disappointment his abruptness gave her. It was as if he was determined that no further familiarity between them should ever be conceived, and it was impossible to recall those moments in the car without a feeling of incredulity.

'I—er—I wanted to ask if it would be all right if I took Anya to Penrith,' she said now, adopting a politeness she was far from feeling. 'There—well, there are things she needs. Shoes, clothes, underwear. Have I your permission to buy her a winter wardrobe? It's something she badly needs. The garments she's wearing at present are rapidly falling to pieces, and——'

'I'm afraid I don't have the time to take you into Penrith today, Miss Seton,' he interrupted her brusquely. 'I appreciate your concern on Anya's behalf, but unfortunately it's not possible for me to take time out for shopping in the middle of a working day.'

'I didn't ask *you* to take time out for shopping,' Joanna replied evenly. 'I merely wanted your permission to borrow the Range Rover and to buy the things Anya needs. I'm quite capable of driving myself to Penrith.'

Jake stared at her broodingly. 'You want to borrow the Range Rover?'

'If you don't mind.'

'Have you ever driven one before?'

'No. But I don't suppose it's any different from a car.'

'I'm afraid it is.' His tone was not encouraging. 'Range Rovers have a four-wheel drive system, the same as Land Rovers.'

Joanna squared her slim shoulders. 'Are you saying that I can't borrow it, then?'

He sighed. 'Miss Seton——'

'We can always take the bus. That is how I came here, after all.'

'You persist in wanting your own way, don't you, Miss Seton? Is it unreasonable that you might accept that although I'm too busy today to pander to your whims, there's every possibility that I shall have to go into Penrith myself before the week is out to get supplies?'

Joanna gasped. 'Is that how you see it? Pandering to *my* whims? Don't you care that your daughter is running around in clothes only fit for a jumble sale!'

'That's an exaggeration, Miss Seton!'

It was, and she knew it. But she hated that look of smug satisfaction on his lean dark face, and she longed to say something to shatter his air of controlled indifference.

'You don't care, do you?' she stormed, saying the first thing that came into her head. 'You really don't care about anyone but yourself. You come up here, cut yourself off from any contact with that hard, cold world that only exists in your imagination, immerse yourself in self-pity ...'

'I think you've said enough, Miss Seton.' With great deliberation he leaned the fork he had been using against the wall of the barn and thrust his hands into the pockets of his dark pants. 'Now, if you'll leave me to get on with my work——'

'Am I to take it you refuse?' she persisted, aware of the tension he was doing his utmost to disguise. 'Is Anya not to have any new clothes?'

His mouth tightened. 'You may make whatever arrangements you like, Miss Seton,' he replied, in a controlled voice. 'However, I think it would be most unwise to use the bus. They're infrequent at best, and it would be unfortunate if you were stranded in Penrith.'

'So, in other words, we can't go!' Joanna's indignation was tinged with disappointment. 'Why? What are you afraid of? Just because you're afraid to meet people, does that condemn us all to the same fate?'

It was an unforgivable thing to say, and as soon as the words were uttered she wished she could retract them. But it was too late; they had been said. And the sudden contortion of his features had a fleeting vulnerability that tore at her heart. But it didn't last long. His fury at her provoking tongue erupted into violent speech, and his response was as destructive as hers.

'What do you know of me—of my feelings?' he grated. 'Do you think because I was once foolish enough to caress that promiscuous body of yours that you know all there is to know about me? What do you know of the world—the real world, I mean, *my* world? Have you ever suffered the torment of knowing you're no good for anything any more? Useless, both to yourself and the people around you? Of course you haven't. You say I don't care about anybody but myself—well, perhaps it's true. But perhaps that's because it's easier on other people that way. Do you think I want anybody's pity? Do you think I want to hear people telling their friends not to mind me, that I'm harmless enough, just a vegetable, left to rot in some round hole I don't fit any more!'

'You don't know that,' she protested urgently, disturbed in spite of herself. 'How do you know how people would react? You haven't given them a chance. How do you honestly know you can't work any more? You don't know something like that until you try.'

'Ever the optimist, aren't you?' he jeered grimly. 'Are you sure Marcia hadn't other plans for you than Anya's education?'

'I don't know what you mean.' Joanna felt helpless in the face of his implacability. 'But if it helps you to rail at me, then go ahead. I don't care. Anything's better than apathy. Just because you lost your wife—because she's dead, and nothing you can do——'

'What?' He lunged towards her, grasping her arm just above the elbow and glaring angrily down at her from their consequent nearness. 'What do you mean? What crazy ideas are you nurturing now?' He shook his head impatiently. 'You poor romantic fool, do you imagine I'm harbouring some hopeless passion for Elizabeth? Do you think it was my grief at losing her that unhinged my mind?'

'It's natural that——'

'Natural rubbish,' he retorted bleakly. 'Obviously, Marcia left out the more salient points of our relationship. Did she not explain that Elizabeth was suing for a divorce? That any affection we'd had for one another died soon after Anya was born.'

Joanna gazed up at him. 'But you have a son as well. A—a nineteen-year-old son. At—at university.'

'Victor is my *step*son, Miss Seton. Elizabeth had already been married and divorced before we met. The boy was seven years old when we—became husband and wife. He now lives with his father's family.'

Joanna felt totally perplexed. Aunt Lydia had not always been accurate in her revelations, and in this instance it appeared she had been completely misled. It explained so many things, of course—the fact that the boy's name was never mentioned, his prolonged absence from the household, and Aunt Lydia's mistaken ideas about Jake's own age.

'I'm sorry,' she said now, aware of the numbing effect his fingers were having on her arm. 'Naturally, I thought——'

'You're not paid to think, Miss Seton,' he essayed, the tawny eyes glittering between their dark fringe of lashes. 'My God, you do persist in stirring up the hornets' nest, don't you? Why, I wonder? Is that how you get your kicks? By destroying what little self-respect I have left?'

'I don't know what you're talking about,' she got out unsteadily. 'There's no point in discussing the matter any longer, Mr Sheldon. You've made your position perfectly clear. And now, if you'll let me go, I'll tell Anya your answer.'

'And damn me in the process,' he suggested roughly, looking down at his fingers, dark against the cream wool of her sweater. 'What do you really want from me, I wonder? *Blood?*'

Almost imperceptibly, the atmosphere in the barn had altered as he spoke, and Joanna was immediately aware of it. It was as if their closeness—his touching her—had wrought some chemical change, and she could tell by the narrowing of his eyes that he was recognising the intimacy. His thumb—at least, she thought it was his thumb—probed the vulnerability of veins protected within the joint of her arm; but even as Joanna strove to remain unmoved by its sensuous exploration, Anya's clear voice rang behind them.

'Miss Seton, Miss Seton! You've got a visitor. It's Mr Trevor.'

Nothing could have been designed to promote a more violent withdrawal. Almost before Anya had finished speaking, Jake's hand had dropped from her arm, and she stood there rubbing the bruised flesh with a sense almost of bereavement. It was as well the barn was shadowy, and Anya's eyes were dazzled from the sunlight outside, or she might have wondered why her father and her governess were standing so close together, and what they had been saying to bring that bloom of colour to Joanna's cheeks.

As it was, she hovered in the open doorway, more intent on feeding the fires of resentment her father would display at the other man's unwelcome arrival, enjoying what she thought was Joanna's embarrassment at Paul's tenacity.

'Did you invite him here?' Jake demanded now, addressing his question to Joanna as he strode towards the door, and she shook her head indignantly.

'No. But there's no reason why he shouldn't come, is there?' She summoned all her small store of composure. 'I—er—I'm glad he has. It means I can apologise.'

Jake halted, brows descending. 'Apologise?' he echoed coldly. 'Forgive me, but I don't understand. Exactly what have you to apologise for?'

'For wasting his time. I—well, I've never contacted him to let him know that—that you managed to find a house-keeper.'

Jake's mouth compressed. 'You can forget it. I myself apprised his father of that fact the day after Mrs Parrish's arrival.'

Joanna gasped. 'And you didn't think to tell me?'

He shrugged. 'I didn't consider it concerned you.'

Joanna knew she ought to keep silent, particularly with Anya's sharp eyes alert for every word, but she couldn't.

'What you mean is, you wanted to deter Paul from coming to Ravengarth! You knew about our bargain, and you hoped he'd take the hint. Well, apparently he hasn't, and I for one am delighted!' And with that, she brushed past both of them, out of the barn and across the yard to where Paul was waiting, leaning against the bonnet of the Land Rover.

'So there you are!' he exclaimed, with evident relief. 'I was beginning to wonder if Sheldon's daughter was just having me on. She said you were in the barn, but I had my suspicions. Don't tell me he's got you doing farm chores now there's someone to look after the house.'

'No.' Joanna forced a smile, but it wasn't easy, particularly as she was aware of Jake and his daughter rapidly approaching behind her. 'I—er—Anya and I—we wanted to go into Penrith shopping, and I went to ask if I could borrow the Range Rover. But I can't.'

Paul's face beamed. 'Well now, isn't that a coincidence? It just so happens I'm going into Penrith this morning. How would you and—and Anya like to ride in with me?'

Joanna opened her mouth to reply, and then closed it again as Jake came abreast of them. His expression told her he had heard Paul's suggestion, and his response was not unexpected.

'That won't be necessary, Trevor,' he remarked, after offering a perfunctory greeting. 'Naturally, if Miss Seton wishes to accompany you, I have no objections, but Anya will stay at home.'

'Oh, Daddy!' Anya's cry was anguished. 'But I want to go! Miss Seton said she'd take me. Why can't I go with Mr Trevor too?'

'Yes, why can't she?' exclaimed Joanna, doing the unforgivable thing and taking the child's part against her father. 'It doesn't matter to you how we get to Penrith, does it? So long as you're not involved.'

Jake's eyes smouldered. 'Mr Trevor can't be expected to welcome the company of an eleven-year-old, Miss Seton,' he retorted, the coldness of his voice belying the amber fire. 'As I say, your time is your own.'

'There's really no reason why she shouldn't come with us, Sheldon,' Paul put in smoothly, and Anya turned an appealing face in her father's direction.

'Please, Daddy,' she begged, tugging at his sleeve, and his expression softened in response to her pleading.

'Very well,' he said at last, though the look he turned on Joanna was not encouraging. 'If Miss Seton insists on making the trip today, instead of later in the week, then I suppose you can go with her.'

'Thank you, Daddy!'

Anya hugged her arm against her cheek, delighted to have won her own way for once, but Joanna knew it was a hollow victory. Jake had deliberately made her the protagonist, and the responsibility for the outing was on her head.

'We'll get our coats,' she said tightly, refusing to give in to his moral blackmail, and with merely a bow of his head in Paul's direction, Jake strode away.

Despite her fears to the contrary, both Joanna and Anya enjoyed the outing. Paul was a talkative companion, and although he got impatient when Anya interrupted their conversation, he endeavoured not to ignore her completely. Anya, Joanna guessed, was simply enjoying the unaccustomed change of surroundings, and with a promise of some new exercise books for her writing, she was more willing to behave herself. The possibility of getting some new clothes was less appealing, but Joanna hoped that once she saw herself in feminine clothes she would begin to show an interest.

They left Paul in the market place, with a promise to meet him in two hours for lunch. He had invited them to join him in the Buttery of the local hotel, and even Anya seemed excited at the prospect. Joanna guessed it was years since the girl had taken a meal in a restaurant, and she half wished Jake had accompanied them.

It didn't take long to locate a shop that specialised in children's clothes, and Joanna was delighted to find it stocked up-to-date as well as traditional items. It was fascinating, looking at the racks of skirt and trouser suits, smocks and pinafores, shirts and waistcoats. There were dresses with matching waistcoats, leather jackets, with fun-fur collars, long-skirted party wear, and jeans for every occasion. Even Anya's reluctant interest was aroused, and pretty soon she was trying on garments with increasing enthusiasm, delighted to discover her skimpy shape was complemented by the most fashionable clothes.

'Mummy used to say I was too thin,' she volunteered, as she stood before the long mirror in a becoming skirt suit of fringed suede, with a contrasting scarlet shirt and boot-lace tie. 'She said girls should be round and chubby, not bony freaks like me.'

Joanna was appalled that the child should have such memories of her mother, but she turned her remarks aside, saying instead: 'These days it's fashionable to be slim. But it really doesn't matter what you are, so long as you're happy. And everyone can look smart. So long as they choose the right clothes.'

Anya nodded. 'I like this suit. It's pretty. Do you think Daddy will like it, too?'

'I'm sure he will,' Joanna assured her, more firmly than she felt. 'We'll have that—and the other trouser suit, the green wool one. And those two dresses you tried on before.'

Anya's eyes widened. 'Gosh! Won't Daddy mind?'

Joanna sighed. 'If he does, he can take the cost for these things out of my wages,' she replied. 'Now, we need some underwear and some boots.'

Anya hesitated, looking at her doubtfully. 'Why should you do this for me?' she asked curiously. 'I mean, you're not my aunt or anything. You're not even related to me.'

Joanna bent her head, making a display of looking for her wallet. 'Let's say I'm willing to speculate on the future,' she said, not quite knowing what she meant by that, but Anya still lingered.

'You mean—my future?' she asked, frowning, and Joanna was forced to meet her gaze.

'What else?' she retorted, controlling her colour with

difficulty. 'Now hurry and get changed. We still have quite a lot to do.'

By the time they met Paul in the Buttery of the Golden Lion they were loaded down with parcels and carrier bags. As well as the items Joanna had purchased at the first shop, there was underwear and nightwear, shirts and sweaters, socks and shoes, and a pair of knee-length leather boots, with a heel that delighted Anya. She was so excited, she spent the first ten minutes telling Paul about the things they had bought, and Joanna reflected, with a certain amount of satisfaction, how much more natural it was for her to chatter on in this way, instead of displaying the sullen insolence she had first encountered. Was it only attention Anya had been lacking? Someone to listen to her and understand her problems? Or was it that since Mrs Harris had departed the atmosphere at Ravengarth had changed, and she had no longer any need to be on the defensive?

When the meal was eventually served and Anya was tucking in to scampi and chips, Paul took time out to ask Joanna how she had been. 'We've been rather concerned about you,' he said, and she hoped Anya wasn't paying him any attention. 'You haven't taken any more walks to the village.'

It was difficult to be frank with the child looking on, but Joanna tried anyway. 'There's been no need,' she explained, glancing at Anya's bent head. 'To go to the village, I mean. Mrs Parrish has her own car. But we have taken walks by the stream, and once we walked as far as Heronsfoot.'

Paul frowned. 'Mrs Parrish,' he mused. 'That's the new housekeeper, I presume. Is she satisfactory?'

'Very satisfactory,' Joanna nodded. 'She's very nice, actually. She's a widow—from a village near here. She has a grown-up family of her own.'

'She makes super pies,' Anya put in at this point, dispelling any suspicion that she had not been listening to their conversation. 'Does your housekeeper make pies, Mr Trevor? If not, you ought to try Mrs Parrish's.'

Paul smiled. 'I don't have a housekeeper, Anya,' he explained. 'I live with my parents, and my mother does all the cooking in our house. You'll have to get Miss Seton to bring you over to sample her cakes one afternoon.' He cast a challenging look in Joanna's direction. 'I'm sure she'll confirm that they're super, too.'

Anya had been listening with evident interest, and now she said: 'You have a farm, don't you? It's bigger than Ravengarth. Do you have horses?'

Joanna's spirits took a distinctive downward trend as Paul assured the girl that indeed they had. And what was more, his father had offered her the chance to ride one of them if she chose to do so.

'Didn't Miss Seton tell you?' he asked, feigning innocence, and it was left to Joanna to soothe Anya's indignant feelings.

'Your father wasn't enthusiastic,' she replied carefully. 'I suppose he was thinking of your welfare. Horses can be dangerous animals—believe me, I know.'

She remembered her father's death with sudden depression. Her life had seemed so simple up to that point. Her mother's, too. Now she was the only breadwinner, and Mrs Seton had become little more than a helpless invalid. She had depended on her husband so much, they both had, and it was hard for Joanna to reconcile the love she had had for Martin Seton all his life with the feelings of helplessness she had experienced upon discovering his reckless disregard for his family's future. He had gambled, and he had lost, and Joanna was only now beginning to forgive him for leaving them to make the best of their lives. It wasn't so bad for her; she was young and resilient. But her mother had never expected to have to beg help from friends and relatives, and only Aunt Lydia's intervention had saved the situation.

'I know how to ride,' Anya was saying proudly. 'I used to have a pony of my own which Daddy kept stabled near town. I used to ride every weekend.' She spoke wistfully now, and then seemed to realise she was dropping her guard. 'Anyway, I'd like to borrow your horse, Mr Trevor. And I'm sure I can persuade Daddy to let me.'

Joanna wished she was as sure, but she refrained from

arguing. She had enough on her mind with the more immediate problems of Anya's new wardrobe, and she wished she had been a little more circumspect in the extent of her purchases.

It was almost four o'clock when Paul dropped them at the gates of Ravengarth. He refused Joanna's offer of a cup of tea, much to her relief, and instead suggested he might call again towards the end of the week.

'I could drive you and Anya over to the farm, instead of leaving you to tramp through the woods,' he said, as an afterthought. 'You might even stay for lunch if you're not busy.'

'Oh, really—I'll let you know,' insisted Joanna firmly. 'That is—Mr Sheldon may not—be enthusiastic.'

'Don't you want to go, Miss Seton?' asked Anya pointedly, and with a slight deepening of colour in her cheeks, Joanna demurred.

'I'll let you know,' she said again, and with a polite wave of her hand urged Anya across the yard and into the house.

Mrs Parrish was in the kitchen, making herself and Matt a pot of tea. She and the old gardener-cum-handyman got along very well in the main, although he was apt to grumble about the amount of logs she had him saw sometimes, and her insistence that he always remove his boots before stepping across her neatly polished floor.

'Well now, what have you got there?' she asked with a twinkle, as Anya carried her parcels into the room and allowed them to tumble all over the table. 'Seems like you've bought up half of Penrith, by the looks of things. I hope your father isn't going to be bankrupt after this extravagance.'

Anya giggled, but Joanna found her own sense of humour somewhat lacking. Mrs Parrish had a habit of saying what she had only been thinking, and in this instance it was too close for comfort.

'Miss Seton paid for everything,' declared Anya, with the inconsequence of youth. 'She said if Daddy didn't want to pay, it didn't matter.'

Mrs Parrish raised her eyebrows at this, and even Matt

looked a trifle doubtful, and Joanna hastened to correct the child's statement. 'I said—if Mr Sheldon objected, he could take the cost out of my wages,' she explained uncomfortably. Then, needing reassurance, she added : 'But you don't think he will, do you? I mean, Anya needed these things.'

They were all still looking at one another, each of them searching for the right response, when Joanna heard footsteps approaching down the hall. It had to be Jake. Either he had been in the house all the time, or he had just come in, she wasn't sure which, but at least she was not to be kept in suspense over her reckless buying spree.

The door opened and he came into the room, his dark visage casting an immediate shadow on the proceedings—or so it seemed to Joanna's anxious mind. His eyes moved swiftly round the room, identifying the four people present, and then turned to Joanna in fleeting interrogation.

'Daddy!' Anya's excited cry broke the silence, and she danced towards him, wrapping her arms around his hips and pressing her small body against him. 'Daddy, we've had a marvellous time! We had lunch with Mr Trevor at a hotel, and we've done heaps of shopping. You're not cross, are you? You don't mind that Miss Seton spent all your money?'

Jake looked down at his daughter with wry cynicism. 'It seems to me it would be all the same if I did,' he remarked dryly, and Joanna tensed at the implied criticism. Then he lifted his head and fixed her with a piercing stare. 'I trust you had a pleasant day, Miss Seton. At least you appear to have succeeded in teaching Anya to appreciate her femininity at last.'

It was a half-hearted compliment at best, but Joanna refused to be intimidated. 'Anya's an easy child to buy for,' she said. 'All the current styles are suited to her size and shape.'

'Miss Seton says I'm not bony, just slim,' averred Anya eagerly. 'Do you think I'm pretty, Daddy? The lady in the shop said I was.'

'And so you are,' exclaimed Mrs Parrish, relieving the situation. 'It'll be a change to see you in something other than those old jeans. You'll look like a proper little girl.'

Jake released himself from his daughter's clinging arms and went to examine the articles spread across the table for himself. 'Miss Seton has certainly been generous,' he remarked, his expression sardonic. 'I just wonder when you're going to wear all these things, Anya. Unlike Miss Seton, the chances of you moving in social circles are decidedly doubtful.'

Joanna's lips tightened, and she wished she had the right to tell him to shut up. It was as if he was determined to belittle her efforts, but in so doing he was destroying his daughter's enthusiasm.

'Anya—Anya might like to spend a weekend with my mother and me,' she flung at him recklessly, ignoring the practicalities of such an invitation. 'When I have a weekend off, she—she could come home with me. It's only a small flat, but she could share my room——'

'I think that is most unlikely,' Jake overrode her harshly, and she knew she had succeeded in dispelling his patronising manner. But in its place was something far more destructive. 'I don't propose to allow Anya to become a curiosity, a figure of fun, for your friends to treat with condescension!'

'And isn't that just what you're doing?' demanded Joanna, aware of Anya's startled gaze, but unable to prevent the instinctive need to defend herself. 'Why should anyone make fun of her? She's a perfectly normal little girl. There's nothing wrong with her that can't be mended, so long as she isn't corrupted by your distorted view of life!'

Matt muttered something about seeing to the milking then, and even Mrs Parrish made an excuse and disappeared into the pantry. It left Joanna alone to face Jake and his daughter, but her taste for the confrontation was rapidly dwindling. Once again, she realised, she had spoken without considering her words, and even Anya looked shocked at her manner of attack.

There was an uneasy silence while Joanna stood there, her face burning, feeling the weight of censure upon her, and then Jake said bleakly:

'I suggest this is neither the time nor the place to discuss

Anya's future.' He paused, long fingers probing his scarred cheek—which did not make Joanna feel any better. 'Later this evening I'll speak to you in the library. Perhaps then we can clarify your position in this household, and consider what means I have at my disposal to—improve the situation.'

Joanna licked her dry lips, but she couldn't remain silent. 'You're going to dismiss me, is that it?' she burst out, wondering what she would do if it were so, and his tawny eyes glittered.

'As I say, we'll discuss these matters later,' he replied, with cold deliberation, and she knew he was not about to satisfy her anxiety.

Anya pursed her lips. 'Don't you like my clothes, Daddy?' she exclaimed, and Joanna realised that for all her maturity in some ways she was still only a child, concerned with more immediate matters. 'It wasn't my idea to spend so much money. But Miss Seton said if you couldn't afford them, you could take the money out of her wages.'

'Really?' Once again Joanna squirmed beneath that contemptuous appraisal. 'Well, I'd hazard a guess that Miss Seton's finances are in a worse state than mine, little one, and if anyone can't afford new clothes, it's Miss Seton.'

Anya looked confused. 'But——'

'The cost of the clothes is not in question,' her father retorted smoothly. 'And now I think it's time you went and washed your hands. You can take these things upstairs later.'

'Yes, Daddy.'

She cast a thoughtful look in Joanna's direction as she left the room, and Joanna wondered what she was thinking. It was obviously strange for her to hear anyone arguing with her father, but, she defended herself, someone had to do it. Someone had to convince Jake Sheldon that he couldn't cut himself off from the world completely. Sooner or later he had to face the future—and himself.

CHAPTER NINE

MRS PARRISH'S reappearance saved Joanna from any further conversation with Jake at that point. The housekeeper exchanged a sympathetic look with the girl as Jake disappeared outside, but although Joanna was grateful, she guessed the older woman had been as shocked at her apparent insensitivity as anyone else.

In her room, Joanna viewed her future with a feeling of depression she could not shake off. It was useless telling herself that her motives had been good. The fact remained that she had spoken crassly in front of his other employees, and he had every right to resent her presumption.

She paced restlessly across the floor, wishing she could learn to hold her tongue. It wasn't the first time she had undermined his influence, and what justification did she have for disparaging his methods of bringing up his daughter?

Dragging a chair to the window, she draped her arm along its back, resting her chin on her knuckles and gazing out broodingly into the darkness. It was a crisp, moonlit evening, the sky already beginning to take on its starry mantle. Yet even so early in the evening she could hear the mournful cry of the barn owl that had made its home in the eaves, and the less eerie, but just as distinctive, barking of the dogs, as they guided Matt back to his cottage. They were nice sounds, homely sounds, sounds she had become accustomed to hearing, and sounds she would miss terribly if she had to go away.

She sighed. Who was she fooling? It wasn't just the cry of an owl, or the barking of dogs, or the bleeting of the sheep she would find so hard to forget. It wasn't even Anya, although the child had begun to find her place in Joanna's affections. It was Jake Sheldon, her employer, the man who had made it abundantly clear that he wanted nothing from her, not even her sympathy.

Yet in spite of everything—his moods and his silences, his cynicism and his anger—she had fallen in love with him, and her vulnerability had placed her in an impossible position. She wanted to talk with him, not fight with him, to share his anxieties, and lean on his strength. But instead they seemed bound on a collision course that no appeal on her part could prevent, with the spectre of his accident like a phantom in the wings. He simply wouldn't listen when she tried to reason with him, and his obstinacy provoked her to say things she afterwards regretted bitterly. But her feelings made a mockery of his self-consciousness about his appearance, and she desperately wanted to convince him that people were not as obtuse as he seemed to think. She loved him. She would have him no other way. But would she ever be able to make him believe it, particularly as he regarded her as little more than an adolescent, with an adolescent's inexperience and immaturity?

By the time she went down for supper Joanna was in a high state of nerves, and they were not improved when Mrs Parrish confided that Matt had apparently gone on another of his drunken binges.

'Got a message from the pub, Mr Sheldon did,' she explained, ladling soup into three earthenware bowls. 'Does he do this often? I wouldn't have expected it of him myself.'

Joanna sighed, fingertips tapping uneasily against the scrubbed pine surface of the table. 'Oh, he—he—I think it happens about once a month,' she murmured absently, wondering whether this meant her interview with Jake would be postponed until tomorrow. 'Did Mr Sheldon say when he'd be back?'

'No. Just said he didn't expect to be long,' Mrs Parrish replied, putting the ladle back into the pan. 'Now, do you went to eat in the dining room as usual? Or will you and Anya just have it here with me?'

'Oh, here, I think,' affirmed Joanna eagerly, unwilling to leave the warmth and comfort of the kitchen for the doubtful heat of the dining room. Of late, she and Anya, and sometimes Jake, if he was at home, had taken supper together in the dining room, but as breakfast and lunch were invariably staggered meals, they were usually eaten in the kitchen. Besides, now that the weather was getting colder the dining room could be a chilly place, despite the generous fire Mrs Parrish always kept supplied.

Now, Joanna seated herself at the table, taking care not to snag her pantyhose on the rough wooden chairs. She had taken particular care with her appearance, in anticipation of her confrontation with her employer, but now it seemed the high-heeled sandals and pencil-slim jersey dress were more likely to go unnoticed. Still, it had been good to dress up for once, and she knew the honey-gold colour of the dress was becoming to the gold-streaked coil of brown silk that was wound like a coronet on top of her head. When she was a little girl her father had told her that one should always go down fighting, and in his own case that had certainly been true, however tragic.

Anya, when she came to join them, looked Joanna over with speculative eyes. 'Are you going out with Mr Trevor?' she enquired, perching on the corner of the table, and Mrs Parrish scooted her off as Joanna made her denial.

'I just felt like—wearing something different,' she said, trying to sound more casual than she felt. 'I thought you might have felt the same.'

'Oh, me?' Anya's lips jutted, as she surveyed the jeans and sweater she had worn to go to Penrith. 'I look all right, don't I? Besides, I couldn't be bothered.'

Joanna sighed. She guessed Jake's attitude had not helped Anya to adjust to her awakening femininity, and without his encouragement she would never become the normal child he expected.

'Where is Daddy?' Anya went on, addressing her question to Mrs Parrish, and the housekeeper explained once again where Jake had gone.

'Oh, Matt!' Anya hunched her shoulders. 'I wish he wouldn't get himself into trouble. Just because his wife died.' She shook her head. 'My daddy's wife died, but he doesn't get drunk all the time.'

Joanna frowned. 'You mean Mrs Coulston died recently?'

'About a year ago,' agreed Anya offhandedly. 'You'd think he'd have got over it by now, wouldn't you?' She grimaced. 'I didn't care when my mother died.' She paused. 'I was *glad*!'

'Anya!'

Both Joanna and Mrs Parrish spoke simultaneously, but the girl didn't flinch.

'Well,' she declared defensively, 'it's true. She didn't care about me, and I didn't care about her!'

Joanna exchanged an anxious look with the housekeeper, then, trying to adopt a soothing tone, she said: 'You don't know that, Anya. You were too young to understand——'

'She was getting a divorce!' asserted Anya indignantly. 'She was going to leave me. You don't do that to people you care about.'

Joanna considered her argument. 'Anya, lots of people get divorced every year. That doesn't mean they don't care about their children. It just means they can't live together any more.'

Anya sniffed, a habit she had almost completely broken during the past few days. 'You don't know anything about it,' she said. 'She was going to live with another man, not Daddy, and there was no room for me. Only—only she drove too fast and almost killed us all!'

Joanna was appalled. Until then, she had imagined, foolishly she now realised, that Jake had been driving the car when the accident took place. But Anya knew the truth, Anya was there; and these revelations might well provide an answer to the problem child she had become since her mother's death.

There was an uneasy silence after Anya had finished speaking, while Joanna sought to assimilate the significance of what she had said. It cast an entirely new light on the whole situation, and she wondered if Jake was aware of his daughter's feelings.

'You mean your mummy was driving the night your daddy got so badly hurt?'

Wrapped in thought, Joanna had almost forgotten Mrs Parrish's presence, but now, as she asked the question, she was forced to acknowledge her. However, Anya surprised them both by performing a sudden *volte-face*.

'I didn't say that,' she declared, avoiding their eyes. 'I said she almost killed us all, but I didn't say when. It—it was another time. Not—not the night Daddy was hurt.'

Joanna's brows descended. She was almost completely convinced that Anya was lying, but she didn't know why. There was no earthly reason why she should lie about the accident, and yet it seemed that she was.

Mrs Parrish, however, merely shrugged her shoulders. 'I'm glad to hear it,' she averred, setting the bowls of soup in front of them. 'Would have been an irony, that would, wouldn't it? Her getting killed, and destroying her husband into the bargain.'

Joanna's eyes were indignant as they sought the housekeeper's. 'Mr Sheldon was not—destroyed, Mrs Parrish,' she exclaimed, the censure audible in her voice. 'As a matter of fact, I see no reason why he shouldn't eventually try to take up his life where he left off.'

'But I thought as how he couldn't,' protested Mrs Parrish, as Joanna glanced impatiently at Anya.

'The kind of—effects he suffered are not usually lasting,' she retorted, unwilling to say much more in the child's presence. She turned her attention back to the housekeeper. 'You shouldn't jump to conclusions, Mrs Parrish. Things are not always as they seem.'

Anya went to bed as usual at about eight-thirty, and Joanna left the drab confines of the living room for the more homely atmosphere of the library. This room, of all the rooms at Ravengarth, seemed to have absorbed a little of the character of its occupants, and sitting in one of the easy chairs on the hearth, she could watch the firelight flickering over the shelves of books and paintings.

On impulse she left her chair to kneel down beside a pile of paintings, giving each of them more attention than she had previously applied. Until then she had regarded them as the careless etchings of an indifferent artist, but now she was forced to revise her opinion. They were not brilliant. She had certainly seen better. But their very simplicity was appealing, and with a very little work they might well be worthy of an exhibition.

She sat back, well pleased with her assessment, wondering whether she knew anyone who might be prepared to give a professional opinion. Surely, among all the people she had known in London there was someone who could advise her, and if not, there was always Aunt Lydia, with her large circle of acquaintances.

Then she sighed. Of course, she could do nothing without Jake's approval, and somehow she knew he would never give it. The last thing he needed was for some imprudent art critic to belittle his efforts, and to succeed in anything, one had first to expose one's vulnerability.

Getting up from her knees, she gathered the paintings together and restored them to their resting place, struggling, as several of the smaller sketches slid out of her grasp. In her attempt to save them, she dislodged the plaited coronet on top of her head, and felt the two braids tumbling on to her shoulders. With a sigh, she acknowledged farewell to her brief spell of sophistication, and with resignation she unthreaded the coils until her hair was a silky curtain about her shoulders.

Then she re-seated herself by the fire, kicking off her sandals and gazing disconsolately into the flames. Jake was such a talented man, she thought, with increasing frustration. If only he could be made to see that he was wasting himself by living this hermit-like existence!

She must have fallen asleep, lulled by the lamplit room and the comforting warmth of the fire, for she was abruptly aroused by the sudden opening and closing of the door. She blinked, still half drowsy from her slumbers, and gazed up in faint alarm into Jake's harsh, uncompromising features.

'What are you doing?' he demanded, almost as if he hadn't invited her to join him there, and her eyes widened in mild indignation.

'You wanted to see me,' she exclaimed, trying to dislodge

the feeling of disorientation she was feeling. 'I've been waiting for you.'

Jake sighed, striding impatiently about the room, dark and forbidding in an unusually elegant suit of black suede, the jacket unbuttoned to reveal a matching waistcoat and white shirt beneath.

'Do you have any idea what time it is?' he exhorted irritably, and she raised her wrist watch to eye level and tried to distinguish the figures. 'It's half past twelve,' he continued, without waiting for her answer. 'Half past twelve, Miss Seton. Hardly the time for an interview, wouldn't you say? Or are you so desperate to be given your notice?'

Joanna pushed her stockinged feet to the floor and groped around with her toes for her sandals. 'I'm not desperate at all, Mr Sheldon,' she declared, refusing to argue with him in this mood. 'I—I'm sorry, I must have fallen asleep.'

Jake stopped his pacing to come and stand on the hearth, hands in the pockets of his jacket, staring broodingly into the glowing embers which were all that remained of the blaze there had been when Joanna sought this refuge. Then, as if irritated by her attempts to reach for her sandals, he turned and kicked them aside, looking down into her surprised face with moody intensity.

Joanna returned that provoking stare for only a few seconds before looking away. She had the uneasy impression that his reaction at finding her here had triggered some latent force inside him, and while she was not afraid of him, she was afraid of betraying herself. Perhaps it would be as well if she left here, she thought unwillingly, as the full realisation of the ambiguity of their relationship brought a tremulous weakening of her knees. He disliked her already, but at least that left her some respect. If he suspected her feelings, he might despise her or worse, pity her.

Getting to her feet, she started in pursuit of her sandals, saying nervously: 'Did—er—did you find Matt? Mrs Parrish told me where you had gone. It does seem a shame——'

'Matt was not involved.'

Jake made the statement flatly, dispassionately, and Joanna halted uncertainly, wondering whether she had made some mistake.

'But——' She searched for words. 'Mrs Parrish said——'

'I know what Mrs Parrish said,' he retorted, with a curious lift of his broad shoulders. 'But she was wrong.'

Joanna blinked. 'I don't understand . . .'

'Don't you?' His eyes were enigmatic. 'I should have thought it was quite simple.'

Joanna sighed. 'You mean Matt didn't—go drinking?'

'So far as I know, he's as sober as a judge.'

Joanna stared at him. 'Then why tell Mrs Parrish——'

'Perhaps I wanted an excuse to go out,' he stated, with a deprecatory twist of his features. 'Can you think of a better reason?'

Joanna dragged her gaze away, looking about her almost blindly for the scattered sandals. She had the definite impression that she should not be here, listening to these revelations, and the sooner she made herself scarce the better.

'You're looking particularly lovely this evening,' he remarked, as she bent to pick up the offending footwear, deciding it would be quicker and easier to carry them, and her heart quickened its beat at the uninvited compliment. 'But then you always look beautiful, don't you, Miss Seton? It's one of the crosses I have to bear.'

Joanna bent her head. 'I think I ought to be going to bed, Mr Sheldon,' she said quietly. 'I—er—do you want to see me in the morning?'

'I want to see you every morning,' he said, making no move towards her, just letting the husky intonation of his attractive voice accomplish more than a physical contact could have done. 'I'd like to wake up every morning and find your head beside me on the pillow—but disregard these observations. They're just the meanderings of a man who's had a little too much to drink.'

Joanna's head jerked back. Was it true? Was that why he had used that excuse to Mrs Parrish? Because he, and not

Matt, had intended to drink more than was good for him?
If it were true, he could certainly hold his liquor better than
the old man, but it had loosened his tongue and relaxed his
inhibitions.

He moved his shoulders in a dismissing gesture now, the
harsh mouth twisting in grim self-deprecation. 'Don't you
believe me?' he asked, allowing his gaze to move intimately
over her shoulders and the undisguised burgeoning of her
breasts, to the narrow waist and shapely hips, and slender
legs beneath. 'I assure you, I had every intention of getting
roaring drunk this evening, only somehow it doesn't seem
to have worked.'

Joanna took an unsteady breath. 'I—I think you have—
had too much to drink, I mean,' she ventured. 'Otherwise
you—you wouldn't be saying these things to me.'

'Wouldn't I?' The tawny eyes smouldered as they returned to her face. 'You were supposed to have got tired
of waiting for me. You were supposed to be in bed. Finding
you here—like this——' he gestured towards her dress and
the toffee-coloured glory of her hair, 'has thrown me off
key, and I don't know how to handle it.'

Joanna glanced over her shoulder at the door. 'Then—
then I suppose it would be better if—if I just went to bed
now, and—and left you to it——'

'No!' Jake's denial seemed wrung from him. 'That is—I
wish you wouldn't. I—what I have to say might as well be
said now as in the morning.'

Joanna licked her dry lips. 'Mr Sheldon——'

'My name is Jake,' he corrected her harshly, his hands
balling in his pockets. 'Can't you use it? At least once? I
want to hear you say it.'

Joanna hesitated. 'Very well—Jake.'

He closed his eyes for a moment, the long lashes curling
with an almost painful vulnerability against his scarred face.
It made her long to reach out and touch him, and her lips
trembled as he opened his eyes.

'Again,' he said huskily. 'Say it again,' and when she did
so, he uttered a groan of anguish.

'Oh, Joanna,' he exclaimed, taking his hands out of his

pockets and clenching them at his sides. 'Why in God's name did you ever have to come to Ravengarth!'

Joanna was as caught up in emotion as he was now, and there was no way she could walk to the door and leave him. She didn't want to leave him, she wanted to stay with him, and if that meant a surrender of her self-respect, then so be it.

'Jake,' she said softly, dropping her sandals again and stepping lightly over the hearth towards him, 'don't you want me here? Is that what you're trying to tell me? Because if it is, I don't believe you.'

'Joanna——' As he spoke his breath fanned her cheek, and she smelt the sweet odour of alcohol. So he had not been lying, she thought in wonder, realising that in spite of the harsh exterior he presented to the world, underneath his emotions were as volatile as they had ever been. 'Joanna, what I want or do not want is not in question here. I—I appreciate all you've done for Anya, of course, and I realise it won't be easy finding someone else with your aptitude for gaining her confidence, but the situation can—cannot continue.'

'Why not?' Joanna moved closer to him, so that the tips of her breasts were just brushing the soft suede of his waistcoat. She knew the delicate perfume she was wearing would rise to his nostrils, and in spite of a certain incredulity at her own audacity, she maintained an air of calm purposefulness. 'Jake, stop fighting me, stop fighting yourself!'

'How?' His voice had harshened, as if he was deliberately trying to introduce anger as a defence against her. 'By letting you say what you like to me? In front of Matt and Mrs Parrish? In front of Anya?'

Joanna put her palms against his lapels, allowing her fingers to slide slowly upward, and as Jake had his back to the fire, there was no backward step he could take. 'Oh, Jake,' she breathed, allowing her tongue to appear in silent provocation, 'please, Jake, don't send me away ...'

His breathing had quickened. She could hear it. It whistled tortuously in his throat, hoarse and laboured. Yet even now he was fighting her, and doing something she had never done to any man before, she reached up and stroked his lips with her own.

His response was uncontrollable, instinctive, an urgent surrender to the needs of his physical self. Sane, sensible thought was suspended, and in its place was wild passionate need. With a moan of capitulation, his hands sought the curving temptation of her hips, compelling her towards him, meeting her softness with the hardened muscles between his thighs. It was the first time she had been so close to him. In the car, the width of the console had prevented any intimate embrace, but now she could feel the swollen length of him against her, and knew that in spite of his attempts to repulse her, he could not hide his urgent need of her.

With his body arousing emotions she had hardly known existed within her, the probing assault of his mouth was the final devastation. Her lips parted beneath the sensual invasion of his, and her arms wound themselves eagerly around his neck, seeking a closer contact.

She was hardly aware of him drawing her down on to the rug beside the fire, or of him unbuttoning his waistcoat so that presently all that was between her and the muscular hardness of his chest was the thin silk of his shirt. She wanted to be pressed against him. She wanted to feel his mouth performing a sensuous seduction of its own, and to feel the warmth and maleness of him thrust against her. She would have liked to be as confident as he was and escape from the enveloping confines of the jersey silk, but instead she submitted to his burning caress, her breasts straining against the fine cloth.

'This is crazy,' he muttered at last, looking down at her with tormented eyes. 'Why in God's name didn't you go to bed? This shouldn't be happening.'

'But it is,' she whispered, reaching up to him, slender fingers exploring the harsh planes of his face, until he caught their teasing softness and turned his mouth into her palm. 'Love me, Jake, love me! Don't pretend you don't want to, because I know you do.'

'You don't know what you're saying,' he protested, clos-

ing his eyes against the alluring demand of her inviting
limbs, and she felt the force of the defences he was trying
to build against her.

'I do, I do,' she told him urgently. 'I want to go to bed,
Jake, but not alone. With you!'

'*No!*' He drew back from her abruptly, squatting on the
floor beside her, combing his hair with demented fingers.
'For God's sake, Joanna, don't make me lose what little
self-respect I have left.'

'Why should it?' With a sound of frustration she struggled on to her knees beside him, resisting his efforts to
escape when she put her hands at the back of his neck. 'Oh,
Jake! Don't keep me away from you. Let me in! Let me
love you. That's all I want to do.'

His eyes were dark with anguish, the tawny irises hidden
beneath a veil of uncertainty. He gazed at her agonisingly,
irresistibly drawn by the lissom beauty he was being
offered, and yet fighting an attraction for which he had no
solution.

'It's no use,' he groaned, getting unsteadily to his feet,
and she almost gave up at the determination in his face. But
she didn't. Getting up too, she faced him fearlessly, making
no move to put into order the hair which he had so pas-
sionately disordered. She just waited, in silence, for him to
make the next move.

He shook his head almost helplessly, dragging his eyes
away from hers, brushing the immaculate legs of his pants
free of any clinging threads from the rug. He was obviously
hoping she would accept his ultimatum and go, but she
didn't, and when he lifted his head she was almost sure she
had won.

'Joanna ...' Her name on his lips was a plea for help, but
she couldn't help him. 'Oh, Joanna!' and with a heavy sigh,
he sought the slender bones of her shoulders as he pulled
her back into his arms.

It was where she wanted to be, where she belonged, she
thought wonderingly, returning the hungry pressure of his
mouth with equal fervour. Nothing else mattered but that
he should go on making love to her, and she gave herself

to him mentally, without fear of his physical possession. She wanted to be a part of him, she wanted him to be a part of her—and if her innocence proved a barrier, it could easily be broken.

She gasped when Jake swung her off her feet and into his arms, the tawny eyes slumbrous now and glazed with emotion. She was not afraid, only apprehensive of her inexperience, but her instincts told her that Jake would never hurt her. He was not that kind of man, and picturing him without the civilising influence of his clothes brought a purely pagan thrill of anticipation. Skin against skin, she thought with satisfaction, and met his probing lips with hers.

He carried her across the room and into the hall, climbing the staircase with a determined tread, as if he was trampling his inhibitions, she thought with momentary uncertainty. What if he regretted this in the morning? she fretted. What if he despised her for taking advantage of him?

But she refused to entertain such drab preconceptions. She loved Jake—and if he did not love her now, she would teach him to do so. He had been hurt and confused, but she would make him whole again, and for now that was as far as she dared to go.

He staggered as he reached the top of the stairs, the effects of the alcohol making his head swim, and Joanna uttered an unwary gasp. It was as uncontrollable as it was audible, and Jake froze, making no move backward or forward. It was as if he was waiting for something to happen, Joanna realised later, and he was not disappointed. Almost instantaneously Anya's bedroom door opened, and her small face appeared, eyes round and apprehensive in the aperture.

'Daddy!' she exclaimed, when she saw him, and his burden. 'What is it? What's happened? Is Miss Seton ill? Why are you carrying her?'

Jake's reaction was slow but deliberate. With unhurried movements he set Joanna on her feet, and she stood there feeling like a reprimanded child beneath his condemning gaze.

'Miss—er—Miss Seton fell asleep downstairs,' he declared, daring her to contradict him. 'But she's wide awake now, as you can see, so she can make her own way to bed.'

It was doubtful which of them was the most confused, Joanna decided bitterly, realising that Anya's advent had accomplished all that Jake's protestations had not. She had reminded him of the past, of everything Joanna tried to erase from his thoughts, and in so doing had destroyed perhaps their only chance of happiness. She didn't have to be told. It was there in his eyes, in his face, in the downward twist of his mouth, and her frustration at her own foolishness in crying out like that filled her with despair.

'Goodnight, Miss Seton,' Jake was saying now, making his way towards his daughter's door. 'We'll talk again in the morning. Come along, Anya, say goodnight. It's much too late and too cold for little girls to be out of bed.'

And for her, too, thought Joanna wearily, closing her door behind her. Not that she felt an outer cold, only an inner one, and the devastating conviction that after this there would be no second chances.

CHAPTER TEN

IF she slept at all, it was doubtful, and she got up the following morning feeling the weight of impending disaster hanging over her. She bathed and dressed in maroon corded pants and a matching silk shirt, and then after securing her hair with a ribbon went downstairs to face her fate.

Mrs Parrish was preparing breakfast in the kitchen with reassuring normality, but Joanna was not deceived. Her question as to Jake's whereabouts procured the information that he had eaten earlier, but her shortlived relief was erased by the further advice that he had left instructions for her to meet him in the library at nine o'clock.

Anya appeared as she was swallowing her second cup of coffee, having refused any of the toast Mrs Parrish had prepared for her, and she found it incredibly difficult to face her after the scene the night before. The fact that the child was wearing one of the dresses they had bought the day before didn't help, and she avoided making any remark that might precipitate an argument. Anya's face was sullen as she took her seat, and her mind was obviously not on her appearance, which seemed to diminish Joanna's hopes that she might have forgotten the previous night's fiasco.

Any hopes she had were shortlived. Not that Anya mentioned that humiliating interlude. She said something far more devastating, and Joanna could only sit and look at her while Mrs Parrish clicked her tongue.

'Whatever are you saying, Anya?' she exclaimed, giving Joanna a half perplexed, half sympathetic look. 'Miss Seton isn't leaving. You must have made a mistake.'

'No, I haven't.' Anya pursed her lips indignantly. 'Daddy told me, last night. He—he said that Miss Seton had to go back to London.'

Mrs Parrish turned a shocked gaze in Joanna's direction. 'Is this true?' she exclaimed. 'Do you have to go back? I—well, it's so unexpected.'

151

'She's just like all the rest,' muttered Anya dourly. 'They all hate it here. They hate me!'

'Anya, that's not true!' Joanna was on her feet in a second. 'I—I——' She sought desperately for something to say that would not betray her situation. 'It's just that—well, your daddy and I don't agree on—on everything.'

'Well, you are apt to speak a little impertinently to him sometimes,' Mrs Parrish inserted doubtfully. 'I mean, you are only an employee, Miss Seton——'

'It's not that!' declared Anya sulkily. 'Daddy doesn't mind. He—he said he admired Miss Seton for speaking her mind.'

'He did?' Joanna said this almost incredulously, and then sobered again as she encountered Anya's brooding stare. 'That is—oh, Anya! I don't want to leave, but perhaps I don't have a choice.'

Anya's expression faltered. 'What do you mean?'

Joanna sighed, wishing she hadn't started this. 'Sometimes—sometimes people just—can't get along.'

'You and Daddy, you mean?'

Joanna hesitated. 'Perhaps.'

'But he likes you. I know he does,' exclaimed Anya vehemently. 'Just because you quarrel sometimes, it doesn't mean you have to leave!'

Joanna spread her hands. 'Anya, it's not that simple.'

The child sniffed. 'I don't believe you.'

Joanna made a helpless gesture. 'Then ask your father. After all, he makes the decisions around here.'

Anya hunched over the plate of cereal Mrs Parrish had put before her and didn't reply. Joanna guessed speaking to her father was a daunting proposition even for her, and with a feeling of desperation she finished her own breakfast and left the table.

She knocked at the library door at five minutes to nine only to find the room empty. Obviously, her employer had not expected her to be early, and she paced anxiously across the floor, arms crossed protectively around her midriff.

Promptly at nine o'clock Jake arrived to join her. He came into the room with a firm decisive tread, and one look at his dark forbidding features was enough to convince Joanna that she would be wasting her time in trying to reason with him. Last night had been a moment out of time, a brief glimpse of the vulnerable man behind the mask. But such a liberty was not to be repeated.

'Miss Seton!' He nodded politely as he closed the door and gestured to the chairs by the desk, where she and Anya normally worked. 'Sit down, won't you? This won't take long.'

Joanna hesitated, then, realising her ability to control her unsteady limbs might more easily be accomplished from the chair, she acquiesced, seating herself on the edge of the cushion, hands twisted tightly together in her lap. Jake did not sit down, however. He merely walked round to the other side of the desk, as if this gave him some sort of an advantage, and faced her with cool, uncompromising eyes.

'You know what I'm going to say, of course,' he remarked without preamble. 'I said as much—last night. Unfortunately, the rest of what happened yesterday evening was —unforgivable, and I think it's in the best interests of all of us if—if we curtail our association forthwith.'

Joanna's nails dug into her palms. 'Is that why you needed a drink so badly?' she asked, forcing an insolence she was far from feeling. 'Because you couldn't say what you had to say sober?'

'I'm sober now, Miss Seton!' Jake's jaw hardened instantly, but she was somewhat reassured by the vehemence of his reaction. 'I prefer not to discuss the events of last evening. I merely wish to obliterate them from my memory, and I wish you would do the same.'

Joanna looked up. 'Why?' Her lips parted. 'Were they so unpleasant?'

'Miss Seton——'

'You called me Joanna last night.'

'Miss Seton,' Jake flexed the muscles of his spine rather wearily, 'I do not propose to argue with you. Last night— last night I'd had too much to drink, as you say. This morning I'm rather more logical.'

Joanna got up from her chair. 'Don't you mean equivocal?' she countered, challenging him. 'You don't really want me to leave. You're just afraid to let me stay. You're afraid I'll become too important to Anya—and to *you*!'

'That's lunacy!' His voice was harsh and grating now. 'For God's sake, what did you read into last night's little fiasco? All right, so I find you physically attractive—that's not so surprising, is it? You're a beautiful young woman, and don't pretend you're not aware of it, because I know you are. Perhaps I did find it difficult to put my feelings into words last evening, but have you thought why that might be so? Other than some great passion you're presuming I feel for you?' He was being insolent now, and her limbs froze. 'Miss Seton, I'm a lonely man. I don't deny it. Who could, living in these surroundings? The idea of dismissing you and starting again with someone else is not appealing, but better that than get involved in some futile, and dangerous, relationship.' When she would have defended herself, he made a silencing gesture and went on: 'Don't deny your behaviour has not been that of someone who imagines she holds a special position. You thought yourself indispensable. Well, you're not, Miss Seton, and I am—dispensing with you.'

'Last night——'

'Oh, for the Lord's sake!' He gazed at her with impatient eyes. 'How many more times? Last night I *wanted* you. There you are, I admit it. But fortunately it didn't happen. Nothing happened. Put it down to experience. For a girl of your age and background, you could certainly use it.'

Joanna was pale now. 'What do you mean?'

His mouth curled. 'You know! You were shaking like a leaf when I carried you upstairs. You're just a baby, Miss Seton. Stick to boys of your own age. You're not ready for the senior league.'

Her fingers stung across his cheek with more force than she had known herself capable. They tingled as she withdrew them, her eyes wide and anxious, waiting for his retaliation, but it didn't come. Not physically, that was.

'Collect your belongings, Miss Seton. I'll drive you to Penrith. And please,' he put his hand to his scarred cheek, 'don't do that again. It hurts like the very devil!'

It was these words that hounded her all the way back to London. She had not thought about his face when she delivered the blow. She had forgotten the vulnerability of grafted skin and bone, and she reviled herself utterly for striking him so forcefully.

And with these thoughts had come others, less obvious, but equally convincing. Had she possibly hurt him in other ways? Had her immature attempts at seduction touched inner wounds, that his pride and arrogance were trying hard to conceal? The isolation of the man tore at her heart, and his complexity left her totally confused.

Leaving had been like tearing herself in half. Both Matt and Mrs Parrish had expressed genuine sorrow at her departure, but Anya, predictably, had not said goodbye. At the last moment, Joanna had considered appealing to him on the child's behalf, but one look at Jake's harsh features had deterred any such plea. He was right; she had brought this on herself. She had begun to consider her position inviolable, without realising that Jake was not like other men. Because of the difficulties with Anya, she had imagined he would not dismiss her. But he had.

Yet, even now, she couldn't entirely believe it had happened. It hardly seemed possible that less than twenty-four hours ago he had been holding her in his arms, making mad passionate love to her. But here she was, aboard the Euston express, without any realisable chance of ever seeing him again. It was impossible, it was incredible, it was soul-destroying.

The apartment Aunt Lydia had found for her mother was in a tower block near Regent's Park. The rent was exorbitant, but Aunt Lydia had made herself responsible for that, and Mrs Seton had accepted the situation without question. Since her husband's death she tended to lean on anyone who offered a shoulder, and Lady Sutton was more capable than most of supporting her. They had been friends since girlhood, and as Lord Sutton's death had left his widow very well provided for, she saw nothing out of the ordinary in aiding a friend in need.

A taxi dropped Joanna at the block of apartments soon after seven o'clock that evening, and after exchanging a good evening with the doorman, she entered the lift and pressed the button for the eighth floor. She hoped her mother was at home. She didn't have a key, and the idea of having to get the caretaker to open up the door for her was not appealing in her fragile state of mind. Gradually, as the day had worn on, and the distance between her and Ravengarth had increased, the full enormity of her position had struck her a numbing blow, and she dreaded the next few days and their inevitable aftermath.

The corridors leading to the units were utilitarian, but the units themselves were well lit and comfortable. Her mother's place had two bedrooms, each with its own bathroom, a living room, a dining room and a kitchen, and an attractive entrance hallway, split into lower and upper levels.

Joanna rang the bell and waited impatiently, her case digging painfully into her fingers. She was irresistibly reminded of her arrival at Ravengarth, and her feelings then, but she refused to indulge herself in sentiment, and determinedly rang the bell again.

There was no one at home, that much became obvious after the fourth ring, and she sighed in frustration. She would have to go downstairs again and get the caretaker to open up, and her spirits sagged as she struggled back to the lifts.

A quarter of an hour later she closed the door behind the caretaker with a sigh of relief and dropped her case in the hall. Then, pushing open the door of the living room, she switched on the lights. The room was warm, indicating that its occupant had not been long away, and Joanna walked to the long windows and looked out on the lighted panorama of the city below her. The luxuriousness of her surroundings after the austerity she had been used to meant nothing to her, and she had to force herself to leave the window and her aching thoughts for the quiet elegance of her bedroom.

She was relaxing in a hot bath when the telephone rang, and at first she was tempted just to let it ring. But her conscience—and the fleeting anticipation that it might conceivably be Jake—brought her out of the water, and wrapping a towel about her, she lifted the receiver beside her bed.

'Yes.'

There was silence for a moment, and then a cultivated, very English voice said: 'Joanna? Joanna, is that you?'

Joanna sighed. 'Yes, Aunt Lydia, it's me. Did you want Mummy?'

'I did, as a matter of fact,' agreed Lady Sutton dryly, 'but at this moment I'm more interested to hear why you're there.'

Joanna caught her lower lip between her teeth. 'I'm back,' she said, rather unnecessarily. 'I've—er— left Ravengarth.'

Her godmother made a sound of impatience. 'Don't be obtuse, Joanna. You know what I mean. Why have you left Ravengarth? I understood from your mother that you and the child were proceeding quite successfully.'

Joanna hesitated. 'Situations change,' she said, trying to sound casual. 'And Mummy's out. Would you know where she might be?'

Lady Sutton was silent for a few moments, then she said firmly: 'I think you'd better come and have dinner with me, Joanna. We can't talk on the telephone, and I should be glad of your company.'

Joanna closed her eyes in dismay. 'Oh, really, Aunt Lydia, I——'

'Don't refuse, Joanna. As a matter of fact, I was going to write to you. About your mother.'

'Mummy?' Joanna's eyes opened wide now. 'Why? What is it? Is something wrong? She's not ill, is she?'

'No more than usual,' replied her godmother dryly. 'Well, will you come? Don't bother to dress. We'll be quite informal.'

A slight bubble of hysteria surged inside Joanna. 'I think I'd better, Aunt Lydia,' she said, glancing down at her towel-clad figure. 'Dress, I mean. I'll be with you in—in an hour.'

'Make it half,' suggested Lady Sutton smoothly, and rang off before Joanna could protest.

She wore a woollen trouser suit, and put her sheepskin jacket over the top. With her hair loose and only the minimum amount of make-up she thought she looked absurdly young, and then decided that in the circumstances it was hardly likely to matter. What a nuisance, though, that Aunt Lydia should ring this evening. The last thing she needed was her godmother's eyes probing the inner corners of her mind. Somehow she would have to think of a reasonable excuse for her departure from Ravengarth, and hope that Jake would not tell his sister the real reason he had dismissed her. She doubted he would, in the circumstances, but Marcia Hunter and Lady Sutton were good friends, and she guessed there would be some speculation whatever happened.

Lady Sutton's town house was in a small square near Lancaster Gate, and Joanna walked the short distance from Cavendish Court. It was a fine but chilly evening, and she missed the Mini she had had, when her father was alive, to run around in. Still, the exercise would be a good preparation, she reflected wearily, anticipating the boring round of employment agencies she would have to make in the morning. Unlike her mother, she would not live on Lady Sutton's charity, and the sooner she got a job the less time she would have for the depression that was steadily eating into her.

Megan Duffield let her in, and smiled sympathetically as she took her coat. Megan was Lady Sutton's maid-cum-companion, and on the butler's night off, she was also the person who answered the door. A middle-aged lady of doubtful years, she had lost her fiancé in the war, and since then she had lived with the Suttons in various capacities.

'Lady Lydia is in the drawing room, Joanna,' she said, the Welsh accent she had brought from Aberystwyth still as sharp as ever, and Joanna thanked her as she crossed the hall to the familiar room. Ever since she could remember, she had been at home at Windsor Square, and she opened the drawing room door with a confidence that belied the staggering burden of her spirits.

She was arrested in the doorway by the realisation that Aunt Lydia was not alone. Another woman, a younger woman, was seated in an armchair at the opposite side of the hearth to her godmother, and both women turned interested eyes in her direction as she stepped rather awkwardly into the room.

The awkwardness was not allowed to last long. With an exclamation of pleasure Lady Sutton rose and came to greet her, and the younger woman's face creased into a polite, anticipatory smile.

'My dear, you look frozen!' Aunt Lydia exclaimed, her perfumed cheek brushing Joanna's. 'Come and sit down, and I'll get you a brandy. You look as though you could do with it.'

Joanna forced a smile in return, and allowed herself to be drawn towards the fireplace, where an artificial log fire was burning convincingly. The younger woman who had been sitting opposite her godmother uncrossed her legs to make way for their approach, and Lady Sutton performed the introductions.

'You've never met Marcia, have you, Joanna?' her godmother asked, as Joanna's nerve endings quivered with shock and disbelief. 'This is my goddaughter, Marcia—Joanna Seton. Joanna, allow me to introduce Mr Sheldon's sister, Mrs Hunter.'

It was obvious that Marcia Hunter had been prepared, but Joanna had not, and her greeting was less than enthusiastic. The last person she had expected—or wanted—to meet here this evening was Jake's sister, but somehow she had to conceal it.

Marcia Hunter was younger than her brother, but only by a year or so, Joanna estimated, with dark good looks, and a slim, if slightly angular, figure. Relaxed, as now, it was impossible to tell exactly how tall she might be, but again Joanna guessed she was probably more than her own height of five feet six. She was elegant, too, her simple but expensive suit had a definite Paris label, and her short straight hair was expertly shaped to her head.

'So you're Joanna,' she said, holding out her hand with a friendly smile. 'I'm delighted to meet you at last. I've heard—such a lot about you.'

'Have you?' Joanna found her voice was slightly husky, but although her godmother gave her a curious look, Marcia seemed to notice nothing amiss, and she hastily subsided into the chair Aunt Lydia had vacated while that lady went to pour her drink.

'Lydia tells me you've left Ravengarth,' Marcia continued, with a little of her brother's candour. 'I'm sorry to hear that. I understood Antonia was responding to you.'

'Oh?' Joanna wished she had more time to assimilate the situation. 'I—where did you hear that?'

'Why, from Jake, of course,' Marcia replied easily. 'We do correspond, you know, if only infrequently. I'm afraid he and I see things differently on the whole, but in this instance we seemed to be in agreement. I hoped you'd made a friend of Antonia. She's a funny little thing, but she is my niece, and I worry about her.'

Joanna bent her head, smoothing her palms over the arms of the chair. So Jake had written to his sister and approved her methods. What of it? It wasn't her methods with Anya of which he disapproved.

'I rang Marcia as soon as I'd spoken to you, Joanna,' her godmother said now, returning with a goblet containing amber liquid, that reminded her irresistibly of Jake's eyes. 'Naturally, we were both disappointed that you felt unable to continue with the position. Mr Sheldon must be at his wits' end with that child.'

Joanna took the glass her godmother offered, and allowed a little of the raw spirit to pass her lips. It burned her throat, but it was warming, and she felt it radiating along her veins like molten fire. It gave her the courage to continue with this conversation, and taking a deep breath she said:

'I doubt if—if Mr Sheldon would see it in that light, Aunt Lydia. As a matter of fact, he asked me to leave. Now, what did you have to tell me about Mummy——'

Lady Sutton spluttered. 'He asked you to leave!' she echoed, disbelievingly, and when Joanna nodded, taking another sip of the brandy, she went on: 'But that's ridiculous! Who else does he propose to employ? I understood the position was hopeless!'

Marcia intervened before Joanna could say anything. 'Why did he ask you to leave, Joanna?' she asked with more astuteness. 'Did something happen? Did you quarrel? Or did you ask him about the accident? I should have warned you, we don't mention it in company.'

Lady Sutton was looking most disturbed, her almost white knot of hair quivering with indignation. 'I'm sure Joanna has more sense than to ask impertinent questions of her employer, Marcia. Besides, I doubt they had much to do with one another outside the schoolroom. A man of your brother's age and a slip of a girl! Hardly a likely combination.'

Joanna could feel the warm colour stealing up her cheeks and hoped her godmother would put it down to the brandy. However, to her relief, Marcia chose to speak again before she could turn to her goddaughter.

'I doubt my brother would allow Joanna a free hand, whatever the circumstances,' she remarked dryly, surprising Joanna by her perception. 'He can be stubborn at times, and he's not too old to notice that your goddaughter is an extremely attractive girl.'

Joanna's flush deepened at this, but fortunately Aunt Lydia was more intent on what Marcia was saying. 'Exactly how old is he, then?' she demanded, holding up her head rather stiffly, only to gasp in astonishment when Marcia told her.

'Thirty-nine!' she exclaimed appalled. 'But you said— Marcia, he has a grown-up son!'

'*Step*son,' Marcia corrected her gently. 'I'm sorry, Lydia, but you haven't been listening to me.'

Lady Sutton found a chair and sat down rather suddenly. 'But thirty-nine, Marcia! Thirty-nine! I imagined he was almost fifty!'

Marcia exchanged a faint smile with Joanna. 'There is a housekeeper,' she said reassuringly. 'A—Mrs Harris, I believe. She was there when Jake bought the house. All very proper, as I told you.'

Joanna licked her lips. 'She—she left, too,' she put in, rather quickly. 'Mrs Harris, that is. There's a new housekeeper now, Mrs Parrish. Aunt Lydia, what do you have to tell me about Mummy?'

'Oh, your mother!' Lady Sutton expelled a heavy sigh, as if what she had to say was of minor importance compared to the news she had just received. 'Joanna, I just wanted to warn you that your mother has found an admirer, and—that, if all goes well, she may be remarrying soon.'

It was a bombshell, and totally unexpected. If Joanna had anticipated anything at all, it was a worrying anxiety that her mother's headaches and vague aches and pains had developed into something more serious, and now, to hear that she was actually entertaining a suitor should have been a relief. But it wasn't. It seemed to underline the uncertainty of her own existence, and she had to fight the feelings of self-pity that threatened to swamp her.

A tap at the door gave them all respite, and at Megan's request Lady Sutton gathered herself sufficiently to attend to some problem in the kitchen. Dinner would be served in fifteen minutes, she averred, as she followed the maid from the room, and Joanna wondered how she would fare, feeling as sick as she did at present. Food was the last thing she needed, and she realised all she really wanted to do was weep. Weep for Anya, weep for Jake—and weep for herself.

With the departure of her godmother she was alone with Jake's sister, however, and more immediate matters presented themselves. Marcia Hunter was not her godmother, and she was watching Joanna with a faintly speculative stare.

'Can you tell me why you really left?' she asked suddenly, surprising Joanna yet again. 'I hoped—well, that you might be good for Jake, but it seems that once again he's defeated me.'

Joanna's eyes darted towards her, and then away again.

'Be good for your brother?' she repeated doubtfully. 'I don't think I understand.'

Marcia sighed, and got to her feet, pacing a trifle restlessly across the floor. 'When Lydia—when your godmother told me about you, I was convinced you were exactly what Antonia needed, what my brother needed. Someone young and vital. Someone who wouldn't be deterred by his arrogance. Oh, yes,' this as Joanna felt bound to protest, 'I know he's arrogant. And cynical. But he's also had the rawest deal of any man I know.'

'Mrs Hunter, please——'

'Oh, call me Marcia, Joanna. We don't have to stand on ceremony here.' She shook her head. 'I only wish I could explain how bloody it's been for him.'

Joanna sighed. 'I think I know that, Mrs—Marcia.'

'Do you? Do you?' The woman looked down at her doubtfully. 'I wonder. I wonder if any of us can appreciate what Jake sacrificed.'

Joanna lifted her head. 'We—I—*did* speak of the accident to him. You were right about that.'

Marcia nodded. 'A terrible affair. Thank God it was Elizabeth who was killed and not Jake. That would have been the final irony.'

Joanna hesitated. Then, unable to resist the question, she said: 'Was—was Elizabeth driving at the time of the accident?' She flushed. 'I don't mean to pry. It—it was just something Anya said.'

'Anya? Oh, Antonia.' Marcia nodded in understanding. 'Yes. Yes, Elizabeth was driving. Recklessly, as it happens. Primarily because Jake wouldn't provide the evidence so that she could divorce him.'

Joanna sank back in her chair. 'And—and Anya?' she murmured, almost inaudibly.

'Oh, she was with them, of course.' Marcia shook her head. 'Poor little thing! She used to worship her mother. It must have been a terrible shock to her to hear that Elizabeth intended to abandon her.'

Joanna stared at her. 'Abandon her?'

'Why, yes.' Marcia nodded. 'The man her mother was

leaving Jake for was a much older individual. A Dutchman, actually. He had stacks of money but no desire for a ready-made family. In consequence, Elizabeth was leaving Antonia to Jake.'

'Then that's why——'

'—she's so wild? Of course.' Marcia nodded again. 'And why she refuses to respond to feminine guidance.'

'Poor Anya!' Joanna was shocked. 'I never guessed.' But it explained why the child had denied being with them on the night of the crash. She could well imagine that the scene that had preceded it was something Anya would like to erase from her memory.

'Poor Jake,' said Marcia now. 'She certainly ruined his life. He used to be so—different. I don't know why he ever married her. She'd already had one husband, one family, and abandoned them. She was such a cold creature. Beautiful—but cold.'

'I expect he loved her,' said Joanna tautly, looking down into the dregs left in her glass. 'People do love—unwisely.'

Marcia looked at her curiously. 'That has a distinctly dolorous ring. Do I detect a personal experience?'

'No. Oh, no.' Joanna managed to adopt a half amused, half protesting tone. 'Heavens, I was only voicing my thoughts aloud. But I do feel for—for Antonia. And for your brother.'

'I believe you do,' said Marcia, with a wry grimace. 'What a pity you couldn't stay the course. I really believe you might have succeeded where everyone else failed. Perhaps I should have a word with Jake. Ask him what game he thinks he's playing.'

'Oh, no—please. I mean—please don't!' Joanna pushed herself to the edge of the seat and deposited her glass on the low table close by. 'Your brother is not the kind of man to respond to—to——'

'Coercion?' Marcia supplied wryly. 'No, I know. But it's not good for Antonia to be pushed about from pillar to post.' She made an apologetic gesture. 'Forgive me, I don't mean to imply that you're either a pillar or a post, but you know what I'm trying to say. There's no stability in the child's life.'

Joanna hesitated. 'Do you think Jake—do you think your brother will return to London eventually?' she asked tightly, hoping her slip had gone unnoticed, and Marcia frowned.

'Who knows? He seems to have convinced himself that he'll never be able to work again. Work at his old job, that is. Personally I think he should try once more. His mental condition was not permanent. The doctors believed the symptoms could be psychosomatic, but no one's ever put it to the test.'

Joanna nodded, but the appearance of Megan to announce that dinner was ready curtailed their conversation, and there was no further opportunity to pursue it.

Mrs Seton was home when Joanna arrived back at the flat; but she was not alone. A man in late middle age was seated on the couch in the living room, sharing the coffee her mother had prepared. They both received a distinct shock at Joanna's appearance, and she had to explain that she had left a note for her mother in her bedroom.

'Of course, I haven't been in there since Charles and I got home,' Mrs Seton said reprovingly, making Joanna feel as if she had deliberately deceived them, and her introduction to Brigadier Lawson was distinctly embarrassing, on both sides. 'Why on earth did you go out as soon as you got home?' her mother persisted impatiently. 'Couldn't you have made do with a sandwich for once? I know there's not a lot in the fridge, but I didn't expect you, did I?'

Joanna sighed. 'Aunt Lydia insisted,' she said, making a strategic withdrawal. 'I'll see you in the morning, Mummy. Goodnight, Brigadier.'

In her own room, she sank down on to the bed exhaustedly. It had been a long day. A long, tiring day, with nothing at the end of it but loneliness and disappointment. Why had she imagined coming home would effect any change? She loved Jake. There was no escaping that fact, and without him there would never be anything but loneliness and disappointment.

CHAPTER ELEVEN

A WEEK later, she viewed her future with no less apprehension. Her efforts to find another job had been met with the same opposition as before, and without the month's salary Jake had paid her, in spite of her protests, she would have been dependent on her mother for every penny. As it was, she used her money frugally, walking or taking buses everywhere she had to go, grateful that her wardrobe at least did not proclaim her the pauper she was. But how long that would last if she did not find another job, she didn't care to speculate, and she was rapidly coming to the conclusion that *any* job would be better than nothing.

She arrived home late one afternoon, about ten days after her return from Ravengarth, feeling particularly depressed. She had just had an interview with the manager of a department store who was recruiting extra staff for the Christmas season, and his deprecation of her lack of experience had left her feeling raw and wounded. She guessed he had enjoyed setting her down, but his remarks about the availability of schoolgirls happy to take a part-time job at half the salary she had expected had struck home, and she was feeling distinctly tearful as she stepped out of the lift at the eighth floor.

The sight of the child sitting disconsolately outside the door of the flat dispelled her own problems, however. She could hardly believe the cross-legged figure was who she thought it was, but as she hastened towards her, Anya looked up, and Joanna knew she was not mistaken.

'Anya! she exclaimed, hurrying towards her, and the girl got obediently to her feet, watching her approach with uneasy defiance.

She didn't look a lot different from the first occasion Joanna had seen her. For one thing, she had reverted to her old boyish clothes, and the torn parka, that had since been

166

replaced by an attractive new red one. Her hair was screwed up beneath the old cap, and her face was streaked, as if in spite of her defiance she was not totally immune to tears. Joanna's heart went out to her, and in her own emotional state she felt more like gathering the child into her arms than admonishing her for running away. For that was what she must have done, though how or why she had found her way to Cavendish Court, Joanna couldn't imagine.

'Hello, Anya,' she said now, adopting a deliberately casual tone. 'Where have you come from?'

Anya sniffed, rubbing her nose with her sleeve. 'I came off the train,' she declared, daring contradiction. 'I travelled all the way by myself.'

Joanna's fingers tightened round her handbag. 'And your father? Does he know where you are?' she probed, knowing full well he would not, and Anya shook her head.

'He went away,' she said, offhandedly. 'He won't be worrying about me. Besides, I wanted to see you. To ask you to come back again.'

Joanna didn't know what to say. This was so unexpected. So unbelievable! And while she was flattered that Anya approved of her sufficiently to make this impulsive journey to London, she guessed that Jake would view the situation with different eyes.

Gathering her thoughts with difficulty, Joanna fumbled in her bag for the key her mother had given her, while Anya continued her explanations. 'I rang the bell, but no one answered,' she said, as Joanna inserted her key in the lock. 'I guessed you were out, so I sat down to wait until you got back.'

Joanna shook her head. She wondered with slight hysteria how her mother would have reacted if she had been at home, or if she had returned to find this pale-faced waif on her doorstep. She was not the type to respond to the poignancy of Anya's situation. Her disparaging comments when Joanna had given her a sketchy explanation of why she had left Ravengarth had been less than encouraging. It was obviously her opinion that she was well out of it, but on the whole Mrs Seton was far too busy with her own affairs to pay too much attention to her daughter.

Now, Joanna breathed a sigh of relief for Brigadier Lawson's persistence. At his invitation, her mother was spending the weekend at his country home in Wiltshire, and in consequence she and Anya would not be interrupted.

'Do you live here alone?' asked the girl, as Joanna went around, switching on lamps and drawing the heavy curtains over the windows. 'It's very nice, isn't it? And lovely and warm. It was cold sitting out in the corridor.'

'I expect it was,' murmured Joanna absently, taking off her coat. 'Anya, what did you mean when you said your father was away? Where is he? When is he coming back? Don't you think I ought to get in touch with him?'

She had to follow Anya, who had wandered out of the living room as she was speaking, and she found the little girl in her bedroom, exclaiming over the furry pyjama case that resided on her bed.

'This is sweet, isn't it?' she said delightedly as Joanna came into the room. 'Does he have a name? Does he share the flat with you?'

'It's my mother's flat, actually,' said Joanna, leaning thoughtfully against the door frame. 'Anya, where's your father? He must have told you where he was going.'

'No, he didn't.' Anya spoke carelessly. 'He hasn't said much at all since you went away. It's been awful—all miserable and everything.' She pulled a face. 'And when I asked him if I could ride Mr Trevor's horse, he was really angry. I thought he was going to explode!' She shrugged. 'Then he went away ...'

Joanna didn't know what to say. Jake's attitude did not surprise her, and yet she would have thought that now her disruptive presence had been removed, he would have had more patience with the child.

'Where's your mother?' Anya asked now. 'Will she be coming back soon? Will she mind if I stay here?'

'Stay here?' echoed Joanna faintly, and then shook her head. Obviously the child would have to stay here tonight, but somehow she would have to get a message to Matt and Mrs Parrish, who would no doubt be half out of their minds with worry at Anya's disappearance. If only there was a telephone! But Ravengarth was not connected to the telephone system, and Jake had had no reason to make contact with the outside world.

'I can stay here, can't I?' Anya was asking now, anxiously, and Joanna reassured her.

'Of course,' she said, moving her shoulders in a helpless gesture. 'You can sleep in my mother's bed—she's away. But first, you must take a bath. However did you get so dirty?'

Anya grimaced, putting down the pyjama case and looking down at herself with critical eyes. 'I 'spect it was the coal wagon,' she volunteered amazingly. 'The driver said he'd give me a lift into Penrith, but it was pretty dirty inside.'

Joanna stared at her incredulously. 'But you said you came on the train. Why didn't you just take the bus into Penrith?' She frowned. 'Incidentally, how did you get the money to pay for your ticket?'

Anya sighed. 'I borrowed it. The money, I mean.'

'You mean you just—took it?'

'I didn't steal it, if that's what you mean,' declared Anya indignantly. 'I—I had some money in a money box, that Aunt Marcia had sent me from time to time. I'm supposed to be saving it, so I borrowed some of that.'

'And the bus?'

'If I'd caught the bus, someone would have seen me and probably sent me back,' explained Anya reluctantly.

'You didn't let anyone know where you were going?' Joanna's worst fears were realised.

'No.'

'Oh, Anya!'

'They won't worry,' the girl exclaimed eagerly. 'Matt will think I've gone to the usual place.'

'The shepherd's hut?'

'Yes.'

'And what if he's already found you're not there?'

'He won't.' Anya hunched her shoulders. 'They won't look for me until tomorrow. Besides, they won't mind when they know I'm with you.'

'If you thought that, why did you cover your tracks so well?' asked Joanna dryly, realising there was no point in sustaining her impatience. 'What I'd like to know is how you knew where to find me.'

Anya pursed her lips. 'I looked in Daddy's desk. I knew he had a letter from you there, when you wrote about the job.'

Joanna shook her head. 'All right, so you found me. But you agree that I have to let Mrs Parrish know where you are right now.'

'If you say so.'

'I do,' Joanna sighed. 'But how?'

Anya shrugged. 'I don't know. But I'm hungry. Do you think I might have something to eat?'

'Oh, of course.'

Belatedly, Joanna realised the child had probably not eaten at all that day, and while Anya tucked into scrambled eggs and bacon, she racked her brains trying to think of some way of contacting Ravengarth.

The solution was obvious when it occurred to her. She was helping Anya dry herself after taking a bath in the blue and gold luxury of her mother's bathroom when the answer provided itself. She would ring Trevor's farm and ask whoever was there to relay the message. Despite Jake's possible anger when he discovered what she had done, his dislike of involving his neighbours in his affairs could be overlooked in this instance.

Mrs Trevor herself answered the phone after Joanna had got the number from Enquiries, but although she was obviously intrigued as to why both Joanna and Anya should be calling from London, she agreed to deliver the message. Joanna rang off before she could ask any more pertinent questions, deciding that Mrs Parrish could handle them as well as she could.

She had left Anya in the bedroom, putting on a pair of her pyjamas. However, when she returned after making the call, she found the girl had crawled between the sheets wearing only the over-sized jacket, and exhaustion had overtaken her. She was fast asleep, and looking down at the weary little face on the pillow, Joanna felt an overwhelming sense of compassion for her. Poor little scrap, she thought tenderly. So small and yet so courageous! Did Jake have any idea how much like him Anya was?

Using the rheostat, she dimmed the lights and left the room, closing the door silently behind her. She guessed Anya would sleep soundly until the morning, and she returned to the living room with the problem of Jake still on her mind, and no realisable means of solving it.

On impulse, she decided to ring Marcia Hunter. Anya was her niece, after all, and it was conceivable that the woman might know where her brother was. She didn't quite know what she was going to say when she eventually did get to speak to him, but she felt an inordinate sense of gratitude towards Anya for creating an opportunity. Even so small an encounter looked like a beacon in the gloom of her despair.

She was fortunate enough to reach Marcia just before she left for a dinner engagement. The older woman seemed surprised and pleased to hear from her, but her reactions changed to amazement when she discovered Joanna's reasons for calling.

'Antonia's with you?' she exclaimed, her voice breaking on a sound that was a mixture of disbelief and amusement. 'Good heavens, Joanna! And Jake doesn't know?'

'That's why I'm ringing you,' explained Joanna quickly. 'I thought you might have some idea where he is, where I might reach him. I think he ought to be told that Anya came to find me.'

'Oh, so do I, my dear,' exclaimed Marcia, with a light laugh. 'Have you tried the apartment? If he's not there, I'm not sure where he might be. But you'll probably reach him in the morning.'

'The apartment!' Joanna's voice mirrored her confusion. 'What apartment? What are you talking about? Do you know where—where Mr Sheldon is?'

'Call him Jake, Joanna—I know that's how you think of him. You let that slip the other day, didn't you? But it wasn't until Jake turned up here that I began to realise how the land lay.'

'Jake—turned up——' Joanna was completely baffled. 'Marcia, I'm afraid I don't know what you're talking about.'

Marcia sighed. 'My dear, surely you knew Jake was in London?'

'*In London?* No!'

'Then why did you ring me?'

Joanna took a deep breath. 'Just on the offchance that you might have heard from him.' She paused. 'I—why—do you know why he's in London?'

'Ostensibly to acquire a new governess for Antonia,' replied Marcia quellingly. 'At least, that's his story.'

Joanna wet her dry lips. 'What do you mean?'

Marcia hesitated. 'I think you ought to talk to Jake about this, Joanna, not me. Try the apartment. He might be there. If he is, you're in luck.'

Joanna shook her head. 'But what apartment?'

'Oh, of course, you don't know, do you?' Marcia paused. 'After Elizabeth died, he sold the house they used to live in in Wimbledon and bought an apartment in town, for himself and Antonia. But as you know, he gave it up and went north. However, he still owns the apartment, and it's where he usually stays if he ever comes to town. It's less— conspicuous than a hotel, if you know what I mean.'

'His face.'

'I knew you'd understand.'

'But it's not that bad!' Joanna made a helpless gesture. 'He's far too selfconscious.'

'I know that, and you know that, but you try convincing Jake.'

'I have,' said Joanna dully. Then: 'Could you give me the number of the apartment, do you think? I—well, I should let him know.'

'Of course. Just a minute.' Marcia put down the phone for a few seconds and then returned with the dialling code and number. 'Good luck,' she said, as she rang off, and Joanna guessed that she would need it.

All the same, she did not immediately ring the flat. After

Marcia had rung off, she sat for several minutes just staring at the phone, wondering if there was any point in exposing that vulnerable side of her once more. Jake was here to find another governess, or at least, Marcia had been told that he was, so why should she disbelieve him? Wouldn't it be simpler all round if she just took Anya home to Ravengarth, and left before he learned what had happened and came looking for her? He was not likely to let Anya change his mind about her, and what possible good could come from inviting further humiliation?

Even so, the temptation was almost irresistible. To speak to him again, maybe even see him again. She wanted to so badly. Could she deprive herself of one last chance?

Yet remembering the last time they had spoken together, she felt her spirits plummet. What was the point of contacting Jake? He had made his feelings blatantly clear. All he had wanted from her was her body, an instrument on which to expunge all his pain and frustration. He didn't love her. She doubted he had ever loved anyone, other than his small daughter, and Elizabeth's defection had destroyed all human feeling inside him. He was not a man, he was a shell, a battle-scarred shell, without spirit or substance.

Nevertheless, argued her conscience, he deserved to be told where his daughter was. It was unfair and inhuman of her to keep such information from him, and no doubt he would arrange to take the child home with him. If he let Anya spend the night here, she could arrange with him to send the child over in a taxi in the morning, and she need not suffer the condemning censure of his impatience at the little girl's disobedience.

With this upholding thought in mind, she dialled the digits Marcia had given her and waited apprehensively for him to answer. The purring buzz went on for several minutes before she realised she was wasting her time, that he was out, and with a feeling of intense and unreasonable disappointment she put down the receiver.

His absence from the apartment promoted the uneasy speculation as to where he might be. Had he managed to find another governess? Was he even at this moment en-

tertaining some young woman to dinner, and assessing her
ability at the same time? But no! Marcia had said he
avoided hotels, and he was hardly likely to invite some
strange woman, young or old, to eat dinner with him.
Then where was he? And why did she feel this ridiculous
sense of betrayal, when she had no earthly reason to expect his fidelity?

When the doorbell rang about half an hour later, she
was already sunk in gloom, and even the possibility that as
she was expecting no visitors it could be an intruder
aroused no sense of alarm inside her. It was probably someone looking for one of the other apartments, she thought
wearily, dragging herself into the hall, and then sucked in
her breath in astonishment and disbelief when she found
Jake on the doorstep. He had filled her thoughts so completely a few minutes ago that she could not at first take
in the realisation that he was actually here, and she gazed
at him open-mouthed, clinging to the door like a raft for
survival.

'I understand Anya's here,' he said, when she made no
move to speak to him or invite him in, and she nodded
almost blankly. 'I'd like to see her if I may. I'm sorry she's
troubled you, and naturally I'll pay for any inconvenience
she's caused. If—if you'll just show me where she is, I'll
take her off your hands.'

'Oh, *Jake*!'

It was too much. After the emotional trauma she had
been through, Joanna's composure just crumbled, and with
a mute nod of her head she turned away and stumbled back
into the living room.

She heard the outer door close and presently Jake's
cushioned tread as he traversed the hall carpet and entered
the living room behind her. She guessed he was looking
about him, absorbing his surroundings, but she remained
where she was, by the window, dislodging the curtain as if
intent on some object outside the lamplit-room.

'Where is she?'

Jake's question was not unexpected, and stifling a sniff
with the back of her hand, she answered him in a low husky
voice. 'She—she's asleep,' she said, anticipating his disapproval. 'She was exhausted. I—I fed her and put her to bed.'

'I see.'

There was silence, and realising she was obliged to be civil to him, she turned, schooling the muscles of her face not to reveal how much his presence disturbed her. It was only then that she noticed how haggard he looked, the dark planes of his face hollowed and weary. He did not look like a man who had just rid himself of a particularly annoying employee, and she guessed Anya's running away had affected him more than he thought. He had evidently shaved in a hurry before coming here, and there were little bloody scars on his chin, but his linen was immaculate, and the dark lounge suit had obviously been made by a master hand. He looked the same, and yet different, more sophisticated, and yet more vulnerable, and in spite of her resentment of his heartless approach, her own emotions were less controllable.

'How—how are you?' she asked, clutching at the banal utterance, in an effort to normalise the situation, but he merely ran probing fingers round the inside of his collar and glanced about with evident impatience.

'I'm all right,' he said shortly, and gaining a little confidence from his unease, she gestured towards the tray of drinks her mother had left on a nearby cabinet.

'Can I offer you a drink, then? Scotch, gin—coffee?'

'I don't want anything.' He moved his shoulders irritably. 'Thank you.'

Joanna's tongue circled her lips. 'Are you sure?'

'Oh, *God*, Joanna! This isn't a social call! I came because Marcia rang and told me Anya was here. Now you tell me she's in bed—asleep!' His sigh was heavy. 'I suppose I'd better go and come back in the morning.'

Joanna's stomach tightened convulsively. 'I—er—don't you think we ought to talk?'

'Talk?' He was wary.

'Yes, talk.' Joanna moved to the couch and determinedly seated herself on its edge. 'Won't you sit down?'

Jake remained where he was, and wishing she was wearing something a little more feminine than a denim shirt and matching jeans, Joanna endeavoured to hide her trepidation.

'Did you—that is—have you found another governess for Anya?'

He was silent for so long that her courage almost completely deserted her. Then, almost grudgingly, he said: 'No.' He paused. 'Why?'

Joanna took an uneven breath. 'But you—that is why you're in London, isn't it?'

'Who told you that?'

'Marcia—that is, your sister, told me you——'

'I thought you didn't know Marcia.'

'I didn't.' Joanna sighed. 'I met her the first night I got back. I had dinner with Aunt Lydia, and she was there.'

'And when did she tell you I was in London?' His eyes darkened. 'Was it your idea or hers that Anya should come here?'

Joanna gasped. 'It was no one's idea! And—and she didn't tell me you were in London. At least, not until I rang her this evening and explained what had happened.'

'Really?' He was sceptical.

'It's true.' Joanna got to her feet then, unable to sit beneath his contemptuous gaze. 'You don't imagine your sister and I have got to know one another that well in so short a space of time?'

'How do I know how long you've known her?'

'Because I don't tell lies!' declared Joanna indignantly.

'So Anya suddenly took it into her head to come looking for you?'

'Yes.' Joanna clenched her fists. 'You don't suppose we contrived this? That Anya should make that dangerous journey alone! In God's name, what kind of a father are you?'

His face twisted. 'An indifferent one, obviously,' he muttered, long fingers massaging the nape of his neck. 'I didn't even know Anya knew where I had gone.'

'She didn't.' Joanna hesitated, and then went on half reluctantly: 'She came to ask me to go back with her. That's all. She'll be as shocked as I was when she learns you're here.'

'Will she?'

'Of course.' Joanna glanced helplessly about her. 'Jake, why don't you sit down and let us discuss this like civilised people——'

'Because I don't feel very civilised,' he snapped, tawny eyes glittering in his ravaged features. 'Joanna, I'm grateful to you for what you've done for Anya, but there's no chance of my taking you back to Ravengarth, no chance at all!'

Joanna felt as if he had hit her. It wasn't so much that the blow was unexpected, rather that it was delivered with such vehemence. She had not known he disliked her quite so much, and the whole bottom seemed to drop out of her world.

Struggling to retain some semblance of self-possession, she sank down on to the couch again, realising her legs were unlikely to support her much longer. All she wanted now was for Jake to go, to leave her to her misery, and she hoped he would not prolong this one-sided combat.

'Joanna . . .' Almost inaudibly, her name came to her ears, and she forced herself to look up at him one last time.

'Yes?' she gulped, her voice breaking as she spoke, and with a groan of anguish he came down on his haunches beside her, grasping her hands in his and burying his face in her palms.

It was unbelievable that he should be doing this, that it should be Jake's dark head bent at her knee, and she trembled violently in the grip of emotions long suppressed. She couldn't move or respond. She just sat there, looking down at him, rapidly coming to the conclusion that she was hallucinating.

'Oh, *Joanna* . . .'

There was that tormented cry again, and she blinked nervously as he lifted his head and impaled her with his smouldering gaze.

'Jake . . .' she began shakily, and then the probing pressure of his mouth smothered the rest of her uncertain speech.

He held her face between his hands so that there was no chance of her escaping him, even had she wanted to. Long fingers probed the hollows of her ears, finding areas of erotic sensitivity, and his lips moulded hers, stroking them apart and invading the moist sweetness within.

Darkness overwhelmed her, and her limbs melted beneath the passionate hunger of his kiss. She was drowning in deep, sensual feeling, and her hands groped for him in eager surrender. His searching mouth made her blood run like fire along her veins, and her inflamed senses aroused a strong sexual awareness that struggled for expression.

The pressure of his thigh against hers made her realise he was on the couch beside her, and hardly aware of what she was doing, she pushed his jacket off his shoulders. It was an instinctive thing, a need to get closer to him, and Jake was too bemused by the responsive softness of her lips to resist her. He slid his arms out of the jacket and allowed it to fall unheeded to the floor, and then pressed her back against the cushions, allowing the whole weight of his body to imprison her.

'Do you know what you're doing?' he groaned, parting the lapels of her shirt and exposing the rose-tipped peaks of her breasts to his hungry gaze. 'Joanna, this wasn't what I intended when I came here.'

'Wasn't it?' She unbuttoned the collar of his shirt with eager familiarity. 'But you don't mind, do you?' Her tongue appeared in sudden anxiety. 'You're not going to send me away again?'

'Send you away——' Jake closed his eyes for a moment and then opened them again to absorb the yielding beauty of her body. 'Joanna, Joanna, I have to tell you. I lied to you ...'

Her brows descended briefly. 'Lied to me?'

'Yes. Oh, yes.' Unable to resist, he bent his head and allowed his tongue to coax her tender nipples to hardness. 'Oh, God, Joanna, I can't let you do this——'

He would have drawn away then, but her arms were suddenly tight around his neck, and her eyes were wide and determined as they gazed up at him.

'You can't stop me,' she exclaimed, resisting his attempts to release himself. 'Jake, what is it? Why are you doing this? What's wrong with me?'

He slumped then, almost knocking the breath out of her as he relaxed on top of her, burying his face in the soft warmth of her neck and cupping her rounded breast with undeniably possessive fingers.

'There's nothing wrong with you,' he muttered heavily. 'Nothing at all. It's me. *Me!* And you know it. How can I—a useless hulk of human refuse—ask you to share my life and my inadequacies? It would be wild enough if I was whole—if I had something to offer you. But I'm not, and I'm too old into the bargain, with a daughter that most women would find daunting in the first place.'

'Oh, Jake ...' Joanna's anxieties dissolved into weak relief. 'Jake, don't be a fool! You know I love you——'

'I know you're infatuated by the idea,' he retorted harshly. 'You probably see yourself as Jane Eyre to my Rochester, but life's not like that.'

Joanna's laughter was soft and tremulous. 'Darling, I don't see you as Mr Rochester at all. And I'm no heroine, as you once pointed out. Why do you find it so hard to believe that I love you for what you are, not for what you might be? Believe it or not, I wouldn't want you any other way.'

Jake levered himself up on his elbow. 'You're crazy——'

'Do you mind?'

He shook his head. 'I can't let you do this. Not yet, at any rate.'

She frowned. 'What do you mean—not yet?'

He sighed, allowing his fingers to play with a strand of her silky hair. 'You haven't asked how I lied to you?'

'Then tell me.'

He hesitated. 'It's not easy.'

'Why not?' Concern darkened her eyes again. 'You're not ill, are you? Oh, Jake, you didn't come to London to see doctors!'

'Calm down, relax ...' He soothed her anxious expression with gentle fingers, and she caught his hand and drew it to her mouth. It was a sensuous arousal, and he was not immune to it, and with a helpless groan he sought her lips with his. They opened beneath his caress, inviting the intimacy he had taught her, and the urgency of her response drove him to the limits of his endurance. 'I want you,' he murmured huskily, his breathing as laboured as hers was, 'but first of all we have to talk, and you're not making it easy.'

Joanna allowed him to draw back from her, but only to the length of her arm away, and with determination he released her lingering fingers. 'Listen to me,' he said, putting tender fingers over her lips, 'I didn't come to London to find a new governess, and I didn't come to have medical treatment either. However, I have seen doctors, I'm not denying that,' and silencing her instinctive reaction, he went on: 'but only to find out exactly how serious my mental block was.'

Joanna moved her head in a helpless gesture, and eventually succeeded in removing his hand. 'I've told you,' she protested, 'it doesn't matter!' but Jake assured her firmly that it did matter to him.

'So what did they say?' she asked at last, when it became obvious he was adamant, and he shrugged his shoulders with characteristic scepticism.

'They told me I'm cured, as cured as I'll ever be, I guess. The fact is, that isn't good enough.'

'Jake——' Joanna's face was perplexed, but once again he silenced her.

'Let's start at the beginning, shall we?' he suggested, drawing the folds of her shirt about her, as if unable to concentrate while her silky flesh was enticing him. 'I came because I had to know the worst, I had to assure myself that there really was no hope, and I guess you could say I wasn't disappointed.'

Joanna felt bereft when he drew back from her, lounging on the couch beside her, his expression growing more remote as he told her what had happened.

'They were very kind. They even suggested I go and see Gordon Blakeney, but they were wasting my time and theirs.'

Joanna shook her head. 'Who is Gordon Blakeney?'

'Blakeney?' Jake looked sideways at her. 'You've heard of Blakeney Electronics, haven't you?'

'You mean—they were the people who used to employ you.'

'That's right.'

'And—you went to see him?'

Jake nodded. 'I did.'

'And?'

He shook his head. 'What do you think?'

'You couldn't get your old job back again.'

His laugh was cynical. 'Oh, Joanna! If only it were that simple.'

'I don't understand.'

'Nor do I. That's the trouble!'

At last she began to see what he was getting at. 'You mean—you couldn't cope with the mechanics of it?'

'Mechanics?' He gave her a wry look. 'We're not talking about mechanics, Joanna. We're talking about electronics. Gordon—he gave me a circuit layout of a new calculator they're designing, and you know what? It was like Greek to me!' He shook his head. 'Greek!'

'Does it matter?'

She looked at him appealingly, and he had to drag his eyes away from the yielding temptation she represented. 'It matters to me,' he said violently. 'It matters to me.'

'Why?'

'Why?' He was forced to look at her then. 'Joanna, don't make this any harder. I have little enough to offer you, God knows, but I thought, if I could take up my work, be able to offer you a decent home, a decent standard of living——'

Joanna stared at him. 'You mean—you mean you came down to London because of me? Because you wanted to prove yourself to *me*!'

'Haven't I just said so?' he muttered heavily. 'God knows, I tried not to think about you, but after you'd gone, I thought I was going out of my mind!'

Joanna shook her head. 'You really came here because of me?'

Jake bent his head. 'What do you want me to do? Draw you a picture?'

'No!' Joanna was near to tears. 'Just—just tell me that you love me. That's the only thing that matters.'

Jake's eyes lingered on the tremulous curve of her mouth. 'You know I love you,' he said, though the words were dragged from him. 'Why the hell else did I send you away?'

Joanna pushed herself towards him, pressing her face into the muscular expanse of his chest, fingers probing the buttons of his shirt. 'That's not a good enough reason for me,' she exclaimed, sniffing uncontrollably. 'Oh, Jake, I won't let you ruin both our lives, just for the sake of a stupid micro-circuit! If we have to live in a barn, I don't care just so long as it's with you, so stop killing yourself and me by being so—so stubborn!'

'You have to give me time,' he muttered huskily, aroused in spite of himself. 'Gordon's given me some work to do—simple stuff, mostly, but it'll prove once and for all what I can or can't do.'

'Let me help you,' she pleaded, lifting her head. 'We can be together——'

'No.'

'What do you mean—no?'

'I mean, I have to do this alone, Joanna. I can't ask you to share my life as it is——'

'You're a fool!' Joanna was desperate now, drawing back from him, aware of the loosened buttons of her shirt, the irresistible allure of her exposed flesh. 'What am I supposed to do while you prove yourself? Wait for you? Hang about here, waiting for something that may never happen—I love you, Jake. I need you.'

'Give me time,' he groaned tautly. 'Joanna——'

'No!' She would prove to him that she could be as stubborn as he was. 'Either you want me or you don't. And if you don't, someone else——'

'No one else,' he commanded savagely, grasping her shoulders and shaking her. 'I couldn't stand that. The thought of you and some other man. Even Trevor——'

'Paul?' Joanna arched her brows. 'Oh, yes, Paul. I wonder how he——'

But she didn't finish the sentence. Unable to resist the combined force of her beauty and his own jealousy, Jake hauled her to him, covering her mouth with his own in a rough, primitive embrace.

'All right,' he said against her lips, his breath almost suffocating her, 'you win. I can't take the chance that you might find someone else in my absence.'

'There is no one else,' she breathed, unbuttoning his shirt so that the hair-roughened skin of his chest was scraping her breasts. 'Mmm, that's nice, isn't it? Hold me. Hold me closer. I never want to be apart from you again.'

'You won't be,' he muttered, turning so that she was lying beside him on the couch. 'That is, if your mother and Aunt Lydia, or even my sister, don't succeed in changing your mind.'

Joanna's slender fingers twined in the hair at his nape. 'Will they change yours?'

Jake gave a helpless shake of his head. 'Where is your mother anyway? What if she comes in and finds us like this?'

'She's away—until Sunday,' murmured Joanna, faint colour invading her cheeks at the idea that had just occurred to her. 'Why don't you stay here tonight, too? It would save you having to come back in the morning.'

Jake's eyes narrowed. 'Is that what you want?'

'Is it what you want?'

His grimace was faintly humorous. 'Oh, Joanna, you know what I want.'

Her breathing was forced and shallow. 'Show me ...'

He hesitated for a moment, his hand running possessively along the inner curve of her thigh, and then, with a muttered denial, he rolled on to his back. 'Joanna, there's no turning back, you know. If—if I make love to you, I shan't let you go.'

'Did I ask you to?'

'But you're so—inexperienced,' he exclaimed harshly, as she levered herself up to look down at him.

'You can change that,' she murmured, her fingers straying daringly over his flat stomach until he imprisoned them against him. 'Let's go to bed, Jake ...'

His expression softened. 'All right.'

With a feeling of unbearable anticipation she scrambled off the couch, but as she went to turn off the lamp, another sound came to her ears. It was the sound of someone crying. *Anya!*

With a startled glance at Jake who had heard the sound, too, she buttoned her shirt and hurried into her mother's bedroom. For an awful moment she thought the child had got out of bed and discovered that her father was here, but it was soon obvious that Anya had just awakened, and that her tears were instigated by fear, not anger.

'Joanna,' she sniffed, when she saw the older girl leaning over the bed. 'Oh, Joanna, I was having an awful nightmare! I—I dreamt that we—Daddy and I—were in the car with Mummy again, and she was trying to kill us all.'

'Honey, don't!' Joanna sank down on to the bed beside her and took one of the little girl's cold hands in both of hers. 'You've been dreaming, that's all. No one's trying to hurt you. You're safe with me. And—and Daddy's here, too.'

'He is?' Anya was evidently delighted. 'Where is he? Can I see him?'

'I'm here, Anya.' Jake came to squat at the other side of the bed, his eyes encountering Joanna's with none of the coldness she had been half afraid of. She remembered too well his reactions when Anya interrupted them before, but this time it was different, and he was letting her know it.

'What are you doing here, Daddy?' Anya asked, in a shrill childish treble, as the demands of the conscious overcame her fear of the subconscious. 'Did Joanna call you? How did you get here so soon?'

'I was already in London,' Jake explained gently, dark and disturbing in his white shirt, the collar still open to reveal the shadow of hair beneath. 'Aunt Marcia knew where to contact me, and she did.'

Anya sighed. 'Did Joanna tell you why I came? Are you very cross with me?'

'I should be,' he averred huskily, glancing at Joanna. 'But in the circumstances, perhaps you did us both a favour.'

Anya frowned. 'Why? Is Joanna coming back with us?'

Jake hesitated. 'And if she is?'

'Terrific!' Anya's mouth lifted.

Jake looked at Joanna again. 'What if I told you she was coming back, but not to be your governess?'

'Not to be?' Anya looked confused. 'But——'

'What if I told you I wanted to marry her?' Jake continued softly. 'Would that make you feel differently?'

Anya was obviously finding it all difficult to absorb. 'Does—does Joanna want to marry you?' she asked, giving the girl a studied look, and Joanna intervened.

'I love you, and I love your father,' she said simply. 'And if your father and I got married you'd have both a mother and father again.'

Anya's mouth trembled. 'I don't think I want a mother,' she said uncertainly. 'Why can't you just be my governess? My friend?'

'A mother should be all those things,' declared Joanna gently. 'Anya, try to understand. Your father is lonely. I'm lonely. And you're lonely, too. Let's make each other happy.'

Anya still looked doubtful. 'Would we be coming back to live in London?'

Jake bent his head. 'Some day, maybe.'

'Would I still have to go to boarding school?'

'Don't you want to go to boarding school?'

'Not much.'

'Then we'd talk about it,' said Joanna practically. 'If you promised to behave yourself, I suppose we might find a day school that would take you.'

'Would you take me to school, Daddy?' asked Anya anxiously. 'Like you used to do?'

Jake smiled. 'If that's what you want.'

'And could we have holidays and things, and wouldn't you mind being seen in public and everything?'

'I'd make sure he didn't,' asserted Joanna firmly, challenging Jake's tawny gaze with her own green ones.

Anya sighed. 'Can I think about it?'

Jake chuckled. 'I think you ought to go to sleep, don't

you? We'll talk about it in the morning, hmm?'

'Are you staying here, too?' asked Anya anxiously, looking up as he got to his feet, and although Joanna held her breath, he nodded.

'Go to sleep,' he said, taking Joanna's arm to lead her from the room. 'I'll see you in the morning.'

Joanna went into the kitchen and Jake followed her. 'Would you like some coffee?' she asked, still half afraid he might have changed his mind, but he shook his head, drawing her possessively back against him.

'All I want is you,' he said, with beguiling sweetness, and this time when he swung her into his arms, there was no drawing back.

Nine months later, Joanna stood at the bedroom window of the apartment near St James's Park, which Jake had bought soon after the accident. Behind her she could hear the running water in the shower, and guessed that Jake would not be long before he joined her. That evening they had given their first dinner party, for Gordon Blakeney and his wife, and it had been a success, and she wrapped her arms about herself with a feeling of almost unbelievable happiness.

The water stopped running and a few minutes later Jake entered their bedroom, dark and disturbingly attractive in his cream bathrobe. Drops of water still sparkled on the silky gleam of his hair, and he tossed the towel he had been carrying on to the floor as he came towards her.

'This is nice,' he murmured, drawing her into his arms, his fingers already busy with the bootlace straps which were all that kept her sheer silk nightgown in place, but at her reluctant protest he bent his lips to her shoulder and allowed her to say huskily:

'It was good, wasn't it? The dinner party, I mean. You enjoyed it?'

Jake lifted his head and grinned down at her. 'I know something I enjoy more,' he told her mischievously, and her lips parted in knowing anticipation. 'But yes, it was a very pleasant evening. I told you you'd like Gordon.'

'I like his wife, too,' said Joanna thoughtfully. 'She's invited me to lunch next week.' She coloured becomingly. 'To discuss family matters.'

Jake's mouth took on a sensual curve as his gaze lowered to the gentle swell of her stomach. 'It's becoming noticeable, isn't it?' he murmured wryly. 'Do you mind?'

'Do you?' she countered softly, and his eyes gave her her answer.

'I love you,' he told her huskily. 'I love everything about you. Most particularly the knowledge of my child growing inside you.'

Joanna gave a breathless little laugh. 'I like it when you talk like that. You sound so—possessive.'

'I am possessive. Haven't you learned that yet?' he demanded, probing her ear-lobe with his teeth. 'Come on, let's go to bed. I don't want to be too exhausted to work tomorrow.'

Joanna tilted her face up to him. 'I told you I could help you,' she teased. 'As soon as you stopped pressuring yourself, you were cured.'

'It was more than that,' he told her gently. 'It was you, your faith in me, in both of us. Without you, I'd never have had the nerve to try.'

Joanna smiled. 'I liked the smallholding, you know.'

'I know you did,' Jake nodded. 'That's why I've bought the farm. It would have been a shame to leave Matt and Mrs Parrish behind. Besides, it's served a dual purpose so far as Matt is concerned. It's removed him from all the memories of his wife that used to haunt him, and Mrs Parrish says she's always wanted to move south.'

Joanna dimpled. 'Well, at least the children won't be deprived of fields, and animals, and fresh air ...'

'The children?' Jake's brow quirked mockingly.

'Well, there will be at least two, won't there?' murmured Joanna defensively. 'Anya and ...'

'And *our* child,' agreed Jake tenderly. 'Oh, love, how did I ever survive without you?'

'You tried to,' she reminded him reprovingly, and he

gathered her closer, so close that she could feel the hard pressure of his hips.

'I was a fool,' he averred, his hands moulding her to him. 'If Anya hadn't chosen to make her wishes known, I might never have had the chance to——'

'Don't!' Joanna laid her fingers over his lips. We owe Anya a lot, I know it.'

'And she owes you,' declared Jake roughly. 'You've restored her faith in herself and in other people.' He nuzzled her cheek. 'Maybe Marcia was more astute than she knew.'

'Well, she wasn't surprised when it happened,' Joanna agreed, stroking his hair back from his forehead. 'It was Mummy who was appalled when I said I was going to become a farmer's wife.'

Jake frowned. 'Didn't you really mind living at Ravengarth?'

Joanna stared up at him. 'You know I didn't.' She paused. 'Why? Are you finding the work too demanding? Would you rather we——'

'No. Oh, no,' Jake reassured her. 'My darling, Gordon's not a philanthropist. He wouldn't keep me on unless I was some use to him. But I have been playing with the idea of doing some freelance work, of making a drawing office at the farm and spending some of the time there. Does that appeal to you?'

Joanna touched her lips to his. 'Wherever you are, I want to be,' she said simply. 'As long as you're happy . . .'

'Oh, I'm happy,' Jake exclaimed, swinging her up in his arms and carrying her to the bed. 'So long as we're together, that's all that really matters. Which reminds me,' he shed his robe and slid on to the bed beside her, 'Marcia's offered to baby-sit. After the baby's born, I mean. She says she'll have both Anya and the baby while we go away together, like we did on our honeymoon. What say we go back to Barbados? Making love on a moonlit beach is definitely to be recommended.'

Joanna gurgled with laughter. 'Anywhere,' she said, allowing him to untie her straps.

Take these 4 best-selling novels FREE

ANNE HAMPSON
gates of steel

ANNE MATHER
sweet revenge

VIOLET WINSPEAR
devil in a silver room

JANET DAILEY
no quarter asked

Harlequin Presents...

Take these 4 best-selling novels FREE

as advertised on TV

That's right! FOUR first-rate Harlequin romance novels by four world renowned authors, FREE, as your introduction to the Harlequin Presents Subscription Plan. Be swept along by these FOUR exciting, poignant and sophisticated novels . . . . Travel to the Mediterranean island of Cyprus in **Anne Hampson**'s "Gates of Steel" . . . to Portugal for **Anne Mather**'s "Sweet Revenge" . . . to France and **Violet Winspear**'s "Devil in a Silver Room" . . . and the sprawling state of Texas for **Janet Dalley**'s "No Quarter Asked."

Join the millions of avid Harlequin readers all over the world who delight in the magic of a really exciting novel. SIX great NEW titles published EACH MONTH! Each month you will get to know exciting, interesting, true-to-life people . . . . You'll be swept to distant lands you've dreamed of visiting . . . . Intrigue, adventure, romance, and the destiny of many lives will thrill you through each Harlequin Presents novel.

Harlequin Presents...

The very finest in romantic fiction

Get all the latest books before they're sold out!
As a Harlequin subscriber you actually receive your personal copies of the latest Presents novels immediately after they come off the press, so you're sure of getting all 6 each month.

Cancel your subscription whenever you wish!
You don't have to buy any minimum number of books. Whenever you decide to stop your subscription just let us know and we'll cancel all further shipments.

Your FREE gift includes

Sweet Revenge by **Anne Mather**
Devil in a Silver Room by **Violet Winspear**
Gates of Steel by **Anne Hampson**
No Quarter Asked by **Janet Dailey**

FREE Gift Certificate
and subscription reservation

Mail this coupon today!

In U.S.A.:
Harlequin Reader Service
MPO Box 707
Niagara Falls, NY 14302

In Canada:
Harlequin Reader Service
649 Ontario Street
Stratford, Ontario
N5A 6W4

Harlequin Reader Service:

Please send me my 4 Harlequin Presents
books free. Also, reserve a subscription to
the 6 new Harlequin Presents novels
published each month. Each month I will
receive 6 new Presents novels at the low
price of $1.50 each [*Total - $9.00 per month*].
There are no shipping and handling or any
other hidden charges. I am free to cancel at
any time, but even if I do, these first 4 books
are still mine to keep absolutely FREE
without any obligation.

_____

NAME   (PLEASE PRINT)

_____

ADDRESS

_____

CITY   STATE / PROV.   ZIP / POSTAL CODE

Offer expires February 28, 1981
Offer not valid to present subscribers   08376

Prices subject to change without notice.